PENGUIN BOOKS
GEORGY GIRL

Margaret Forster was born in Carlisle in 1938. From the County High School she won an Open Scholarship to Somerville College, Oxford, where she took a degree in history. Her many novels include *Private Papers*, *Mother Can You Hear Me?*, *Have the Men Had Enough?*, which was shortlisted for the 1989 *Sunday Express* Book of the Year Award, *Lady's Maid* and *The Battle for Christabel*. All are published by Penguin. She is also the author of a biography of Bonnie Prince Charlie, *The Rash Adventurer* (1973), a highly praised 'autobiography' of Thackeray that was published in 1978, and *Significant Sisters* (1986), which traces the lives and careers of eight pioneering women. Her other works of non-fiction include a biography of Elizabeth Barrett Browning, which won the Royal Society of Literature's Award for 1988 under the Heinemann bequest, a selection of Elizabeth Barrett Browning's poetry and, most recently, a biography of Daphne du Maurier.

Margaret Forster lives in London. She is married to writer and broadcaster Hunter Davies and has three children.

Margaret Forster

Georgy Girl

Penguin Books

PENGUIN BOOKS

Published by the Penguin Group
Penguin Books Ltd, 27 Wrights Lane, London W8 5TZ, England
Penguin Books USA Inc., 375 Hudson Street, New York, New York 10014, USA
Penguin Books Australia Ltd, Ringwood, Victoria, Australia
Penguin Books Canada Ltd, 10 Alcorn Avenue, Toronto, Ontario, Canada M4V 3B2
Penguin Books (NZ) Ltd, 182–190 Wairau Road, Auckland 10, New Zealand

Penguin Books Ltd, Registered Offices: Harmondsworth, Middlesex, England

First published by Martin Secker & Warburg Ltd 1965
Published in Penguin Books 1978
10 9 8 7 6

Copyright © Margaret Forster, 1965
All rights reserved

Printed in England by Clays Ltd, St Ives plc
Set in Intertype Plantin

For my mother and father

Chapter One

Ted laid out the suit on his bed. The trousers were creased, in spite of the new plastic coat hangers that were supposed to make sure they remained in the rigid folds he arranged with such loving care. Deftly, he whipped out the ironing board he kept in the bathroom for just such emergencies and propping it up, trotted off busily to the bed under which he kept the iron. Doris didn't like him keeping it there, and neither of course did Mrs L., but James said he didn't give a damn so it was all right.

While the iron was heating, he examined the waistcoat and jacket of the suit. They were O.K. No buttons off and no specks of dirt. Nothing to be done there, so he had time to get a shirt out of the drawer and put the cuff links in. He chose a pair of silver ones. Mrs L. said there was a hint of silver thread in the suit which should be brought out by cuff links and tie. Personally, Ted couldn't see any silver thread, but anything for the sake of peace.

He pressed the trousers carefully. They weren't to his taste. When finally rejected after a couple more wearings, he wouldn't bother with them, they could be sent to some charity when the label had been cut out. This had to be done because they were very special labels with James's name on them, and a little literature explaining that the garment was made for him to an approved design. Mrs L. said it wasn't fair to the tailor to let his things be given to some refugee if it said inside that they were made for James Leamington. She thought it compromising.

When he thought about it, which he was doing as he ironed, there weren't really many of James's suits that Ted did care for. It seemed funny somehow. James was a lot taller and a lot fatter, which maybe explained why he picked what Ted thought very quiet suits. They had no go in them at all, not like their owner.

James was all go and always had been, which was why he went on being rich. But Ted and he were very alike in other ways, suits apart. They both liked football, cars, television and the music hall as it used to be.

James picked Ted up at a music hall. He came to see a little blonde juggler and happened to sit next to Ted, who hadn't come to see anyone in particular. He was what he called 'on spec'. Ted noticed James, which wasn't surprising as James was very imposing looking, and James noticed Ted, which was surprising because Ted was very ordinary. He was small, seedy and at that time thin because it was 1935 and he was out of work. James wore a beautiful fur coat and a rakish hat tilted over one eye. Ted didn't have a coat of any sort and he had momentarily removed his hat because he had a fixation about not being able to hear properly with it on.

They didn't speak during the performances. Ted was too busy thinking what a wicked waste of money his seat was, and James was all keyed up waiting for the blonde juggler. But at the end they happened to go out together and Ted sort of followed the toff he'd been sitting beside partly because he'd nothing better to do and partly to see what sort of car he had. He looked rich enough and dashing enough to be a car man.

The toff went round to the stage door and hung around a bit until he appeared to get fed up and handing a card to the door-keeper walked briskly off. Ted followed. The car was round the side of the theatre, a big Rover with shiny red upholstery. Ted wanted the car so much that all the saliva rushed into his mouth with desire and he had to spit to get rid of it. It was a very noisy spit. The toff turned round and said 'Are you spitting at me?' and Ted almost said 'Yes, what you gonna do abaht it' but luckily changed his mind and said 'No'. Instead he said what a lovely car it was and the toff was all agreeable and offered him a ride which Ted accepted without any ill feeling whatsoever.

Ted finished ironing the trousers and laid them out flat beside the jacket. James was coming home to change after lunch before he went to the races and would be in a great hurry. Whether he would get an invite to the races or not Ted wasn't sure. He wondered if he should go and get his own clothes ready, but decided that would be tempting fate. He checked everything was ready, then went to the kichen where Doris was shelling peas.

'What you shellin' peas for?' he said.

'To eat.'

'What's wrong wiv tins?'

'You ask Mrs L.'

'Get on, she don't know the difference.'

'Don't she though,' said Doris significantly.

Ted took a few and settled himself in a chair beside the fire. It wasn't a modern kitchen though it had all the latest equipment. Mrs L. liked cosy kitchens and was proud of all the copper kettles and the rocking chair and open fire and the red tiled floor and the Welsh dresser with its rows of willow pattern plates. He leaned back in his chair and put his feet up, smugly reflecting that there was nothing left for him to do except wait for James to come home. No wonder he'd got as fat as an old horse put out to grass, though not as fat as James. He squinted at the cuckoo clock – only eleven. Most mornings he was finished by eleven and then slept in front of the fire or went down to put a bet on.

'Where's George?' he asked, looking for diversion. 'I don't hear no thumping around.'

'I don't know I'm sure,' said Doris, primly. Eleven in the morning was one of her bad times with the lunch just coming on. He didn't expect her to be amiable.

He wondered whether he had the energy to go upstairs and see if George was there and ask her why it was so quiet. But she'd only give him a short answer so what was the point. She got worse and worse, none of James's charm at all.

Sometimes Ted forgot Georgina was his daughter and not James's. She was his gift to James in a way, his living sacrifice on the altar of gratitude he'd erected. When she'd been born Ted had been bitterly disappointed. It would have been so much more impressive to make over a son. Then of course there was the problem of names – he couldn't call a girl Jamesa or even Jamesina. It sounded heathen. Nor did he want to call her Ellen after Mrs L. because it was really nothing to do with her, the homage

9

was all James's. Luckily, he discovered James had two other names – George and Charles – so he'd called his daughter Georgina Caroline and been very satisfied

George hated her name. Sometimes Ted suspected she hated James too, which was dreadful because he'd done so much for her. Too much. He'd petted and spoiled her right from a little thing, and then sent her to a posh boarding school and lavished everything on her. When she left school – James picked her up in his Rolls – he'd sent her to Switzerland for a year then asked her what she wanted to do, the world was hers.

'If you've nothing better to do,' said Doris, 'you could take that dog for a walk.'

'I've been run off me feet all morning,' Ted said in self-defence. 'That suit of his was in a shocking state.'

'Don't give me that,' said Doris, beginning to pant a little with exertion. She always panicked two hours before lunch was due on the table. 'I want you out of my kitchen anyway. A kitchen's no place for a man at this time of the morning, or any other time for that matter.'

Ted let the implied insult roll off him. She was always trying to make him feel ashamed of his job, as though looking after James was anything to be ashamed of. Every now and again they would have a real row and she would scream at him that he'd never dirtied his hands since she married him. Well, he hadn't. His job was a clean job. As James's valet he looked after clothes and he had to be clean. He couldn't make out why she should want him to go and get some filthy job, as though there was some sort of virtue in dirt. He knew when he was lucky, which was more than she did. He had a soft job, free accommodation, good wages, lifelong security and, above all, constant access to James.

He decided he'd go and see if George was upstairs. She didn't live there, she had what Ted privately thought a disgusting hovel over Battersea way. But she held her dancing and music classes upstairs in the front drawing room. It was a huge room with two floor to ceiling windows and James had had one whole wall made into a huge mirror so that the pupils learning ballet could watch themselves.

He went up, ignoring Doris's query as to where he was going, and at first he thought she'd been right, George hadn't come. The room was empty, all the chairs neatly arranged round the side, and the curtains were half drawn. He walked across, preening himself sideways in the mirror, and pulled them back.

'Do you mind leaving those curtains? It happens to be my room.'

He turned and saw George sitting by the piano in her leather coat. She had her hair in a pony's tail and her glasses on too.

'You look a mess,' he said, in a friendly way.

'Thanks.'

'I don't know why you wear that horrible coat. I don't know why James let you spend his money on it, I don't really.'

'I happen to like this coat,' she said, and let her glasses fall to the end of her nose, then slumped over the piano and began to play a nursery rhyme in a sprightly fashion. She pursed her lips, raised her eyebrows, and swayed to and fro in time to the staccato notes. Ted laughed.

'You're a proper comic,' he said, chuckling.

'I am, amn't I?' agreed George brightly. Then she stopped suddenly and said, 'Got a cig.?'

'Downstairs, not here,' said Ted.

'Well, nip into James's room and get one of his.'

'Now George, that's enough of that,' said Ted warningly. 'If you want one that badly you can come down and get one.' She didn't move. 'You're a lazy faggot. Aren't you going to go?'

'No. I'm off actually.'

'Haven't you had a class this morning?'

'Sent them all home.'

'Did you ask James?'

'No. What the hell has it to do with James?'

Ted evaded that one. He recognized provocation when he saw it. Instead, he said he was going back to the kitchen where it was warm and he supposed he'd be seeing her.

She waited until he'd gone, then got up and drew the curtains he'd just officiously parted. It was a dull March morning and there wasn't much light. She pressed down all the white keys of the piano one by one, viciously, and then all the blacks. When she'd run through the keyboard several times, she slammed the lid down and started doing exercises in front of the mirror. Then, hands in pockets, she went to one of the windows and looked out.

Her father was just going out into the street, at the double, to open the car door for James. It was his proud boast that he knew the sound of the engine when it was turning into the square and had never yet failed to be standing there to welcome his master home. James got out of the car, slowly because he was now a rather corpulent as well as a tall man and he took a lot of unpacking. He clapped Ted on the back, while making some remark about his faithful gun dog. They went into the house arm in arm, Ted's neck glowing bright red.

There was a chance James might come to have a snoop, so George picked up her bag and prepared to make a quick getaway. She listened at the top of the stairs until the two of them had left the hall then ran quickly down, keeping well into the wall. James came out of the dining room and back into the hall just as she reached the front door.

'Heh, Georgy-porgy!' he said loudly.

'Hello, Jimsy-Wimsy,' returned George stoically.

'Come and have a drink.'

It was a command. George followed him in. Her father was busy pouring out drinks.

'Take your coat off then,' said James. 'My God, it's like a suit of armour. George of England, eh?' He roared.

'I'd rather keep it on,' said George. Ted frowned.

'No, no – take it off. I want to see a bit more of my little girl. That's better. Why hide a lovely figure in that old thing.'

Underneath her beloved coat, George was wearing a brown pleated skirt and a green sweater, very long and loose.

'What the devil are you losing yourself in that for?' said James, fingering the sweater. 'Why don't you buy one the proper size? No man's going to look twice at you hidden in that. Here, get yourself one five sizes smaller, show off your bust. What's the matter, you're not ashamed of it are you?' He took some notes out of his wallet and handed them to her.

'Thank James, Georgina,' said Ted.

'Thank you, James,' said George.

'Well, remember what I said,' said James. He looked at his watch. 'If we're going to see the first race, Parkin, we'd better hurry into lunch, hadn't we?'

Ted glowed, and George realized he'd been fretting all morning about whether he would be asked or not. James liked to keep the whip hand.

George walked to Knightsbridge tube, and then decided just as she was going under that she'd walk all the way home to Battersea Park. It was miles and would take her hours, especially as she would keep stopping to have cups of coffee. It would tire her out and make her feel she'd done something instead of just mooch around between the flat and home.

She walked briskly past Harrods and Harvey Nichols, swinging her bag and bumping into as many of the smart shoppers as possible. One fragile specimen, teetering along on very spindly high heels and drawing a cloud of rose pink mohair round her, received a vicious slap in the region of the navel from George's bag.

'Sorry, old bean,' said George, as heartily as possible. The woman was prepared to be angry, but when she connected the bag with George she contented herself with a derisive smile. George stood still and watched her go into the shop.

There was a model in the window wearing a wisp of pale yellow chiffon – a backless and almost frontless cocktail dress with a tight narrow skirt and its own matching stole draped dramatically over one minute bare shoulder. The wig was a black bouffant style. It reminded George that she needed a new dress for James's birthday party.

As she strode on, she played with the image of herself in the yellow dress. It would undoubtedly bring the house down and settle once and for all her reputation for being the wag to end all wags. She could just see herself, one enormous Olympian shoulder rising in a great heave from out of the flimsy stole, and her back bulging in a freckled mass above the delicate folds of the waist. Before her would sail her be-ribboned bosom and to cap the lot she would sport a lorgnette and the most fearsome of buns – or perhaps, better still, have her hair loose in flowing waves.

George laughed out loud, a great guffaw, the tears pricking behind her eyes. She didn't see how she could ever stop looking like a caricature. It was something to do with her face being too long and big and her damned hair being the way it was. As ever, she struggled with herself not to give way to self-pity. She had to try to alter herself. Pushing to the back of her mind a vivid picture of all the other times she'd had a 'Resurrect George' campaign, she bit her lip, frowned, and wondered what she could do.

She stood and looked in the window of a hair salon. It was very posh, and was called 'Hair by Herbert'. A spindly receptionist, cool and aloof in mauve nylon, patted her own exotic coiffure and gazed contemptuously out at George, which did the trick.

'If you're waiting for someone, please have a seat,' said the receptionist. She waved a hand graciously to one of the mauve and white striped chairs.

'Why should you think that?' said George.

'I beg your pardon?'

'Why did you automatically think I was waiting for someone? Didn't you expect me to be a customer myself?'

The receptionist froze. Conversation didn't come within the strictly marked limits of her role in life.

'I don't know, I'm sure,' she said severely.

'Well, I am a customer.'

'What do you wish?' said the girl frigidly.

'My hair done, of course.'

'Done?' echoed the girl, and then, surveying her fingertips, 'What exactly did Madam want done with it? Shampoo and set? Cut? Styled?'

'The lot,' said George.

'When would you like an appointment?' said the girl disbelievingly.

'Now,' said George.

The girl slammed the book shut.

'I'm afraid we have nothing today,' she said, 'we're booked a long way in advance.'

George frowned. If she didn't have it done now she never would. She stood uncertainly, swinging her bag and biting her lip. A young man with hair that looked as though a mouse had been at it came rushing in. The receptionist sat up, smartly.

'Where's my client? I've been waiting a whole two minutes and I'm getting just a teeny bit angry.'

'She hasn't turned up, Monsieur Herbert.'

'I can see that dear – who is it? Anyone? Let me see – my God, I've never heard of her. For a regular I might wait an itsy-witsy bit, but for a casual ...'

Bert shuddered with distaste.

'Can you take me instead?' said George. Bert appealed to her. The receptionist looked horrified but Monsieur Herbert nodded and swept George with him into his salon, conjuring up a girl as he went to find her an overall. George had to take her coat off and struggle into a flimsy creation of be-frilled blue nylon that did up at the back. On George's broad back the strings snapped. The junior giggled, and said she would have to leave Madam open. Open, George strode through the ranks of women to the empty chair indicated. She sat down and glared at herself in the mirror.

She looked terrible. There was a long drop on her long nose and she didn't have a handkerchief. Surreptitiously she glanced round and found the whole row looking at her. Their expressions were languid and bored but indescribably elegant. George drew a corner of her smock across the end of her nose and the last remaining string burst at the back.

Herbert suddenly appeared in the mirror. George rehearsed what she would say about how she wanted her hair done, but he wasn't interested. Solemnly, the maestro removed the grubby piece of black ribbon adorning her pony tail, and gravely unravelled the elastic band underneath. He held out his hand to the junior who stood at his side with a loaded tray. 'Scalpel,' thought George.

'Comb,' said Herbert.

He combed George's long hair, long enough to sit on. He combed it for hours, clearly thinking hard. George's head ached as she sat watching the straw-like strands flutter between the teeth of the comb. At last, Herbert made his decision.

'Scissors,' he commanded.

George froze. She didn't dare interrupt, but she couldn't bear the thought of having her hair cut – she would look a fright. But then she looked a fright anyway, that's why she was there. Herbert's scissors snipped and six inches fell to the ground, to be instantly whisked away by an invisible brush in case it got in the way of Herbert's feet. He'd left a good twenty inches of hair.

The hospital feeling continued as George was led away to have her hair washed. She ended up lying nearly flat on her back with her neck resting on what felt like a guillotine block. No one spoke to her. All around she could hear juniors and clients chattering happily but she had nothing to say. Herbert, when he re-appeared, wasn't wasting much time. He got through a gigantic pile of rollers in about ten minutes, whisking hair round them and laying them against George's scalp as though they were railway lines. When the last was rigidly in place he crowned the edifice with a length of net after spraying it with a solution that smelt vile enough to be an insecticide.

The time under the dryer passed agonizingly slowly. George sat and thought about what she would look like. Stupid. Jos would laugh and make some crass remark that would make her cry and then spend all evening apologizing, while Meredith would look on her with her superior smile. Maybe not. Maybe she would be transformed and Jos would say he never knew she could look like that. She had to stop herself dreaming such slushy dreams. No miracles were to be expected. All she wanted was to look *reasonable*.

Her heart pounded as Herbert undid the rollers and reached for a brush. He spent hours on the back and she could see nothing. Then he got going on the sides and swept a great wave down on to her forehead. Her face was flushed from the dryer. A big, red, farmhouse face with this absurd frizz on top, like a great slab of congealed butter.

Everyone was laughing. She could feel them. The junior tittered when she tipped her and the receptionist's face said 'I told you so.' In the street people looked at her and laughed, she knew they did. She put her coat collar up and tried to run her hands through the mound on top of her head, but it refused to be disarranged. It looked terrible, terrible. She had to do something, get rid of it before she met someone she knew. She dashed down into a lavatory and rushed across to the washbasin and turned the cold tap full on until the basin was full. Someone asked her if she was all right. She plunged her head into the water again and again until she could feel it giving way, the sticky mass parting and sagging. By that time she had an audience. When should she take the hat round? She seized a comb and drew it through the soggy mess until her own hair stared at her again – straight, lank and only a little shorter. She took two clips from her bag and clipped the whole lot back behind each ear. There was bound to be a Woolworth's not far off where she could buy a ribbon.

George's flat was in a small, decadent square in Battersea, just off Battersea Park Road. There was a triangle of grass in the middle of the square, fenced in with iron railings and with no visible means of entry. Nothing grew there to make it so sacred.

There were four flats in the house. George's was at the top – two rooms and a kitchen which she shared with Meredith and where Meredith and Jos were planning to live when they got married, if they ever did. No one had worried yet about where George was going to go. George had found the flat and cleaned it up and decorated it and then Meredith had deigned to move in.

Meredith's real name was Mary, but she wasn't having any of that. She needed something much more original and pretty, so she chose Meredith and it sounded suitably soft and caressing on the lips of her numerous boyfriends. She and George had nothing whatsoever in common, except music, but sharing a flat worked because George laboured under the illusion that Meredith was divinely beautiful, extremely witty and very clever and that she, George, was lucky to have such a light in her life.

'Where've you been?' said Meredith as George came in with her sopping hair.

'The baths,' said George. 'I'm training to be an Olympic swimmer. This man came up to me in the street – he was a Scotsman actually – and said, "By God, lassie, ye've a fine pair of shoulders on ye," and I said – '

'Oh shut up,' said Meredith, 'there's no salt.'

'Close your eyes and I'll make some. Just give me time to get my bunsen burner – '

'I'm going to be late,' said Meredith.

'What's that got to do with salt?'

'Nothing. The salt's for the chips Jos is going to bring for our supper. He'll be furious if there isn't any.'

'Get some on your way then.'

'No time.'

'All right. I'll get some.'

'Good. Took you long enough to offer. Here, hold my coat while I find my gloves. Ta. How do I look?'

'Sensational.'

'No, really.'

'Sensational.'

'Oh, George, you're hopeless.'

She dithered around while George's huge bulk blocked the door. She supposed that to George anyone looked sensational compared with herself, but she wished she wouldn't be so mournful about it. Jos said really, she wasn't bad-looking, but then he was very kind.

'What time's Jos coming?' shouted George as Meredith retreated down the stairs.

'Seven.'

'What time will you be back?'

'Eight. Keep him happy.' Meredith thought how nice it was to be able to say that sort of thing to one's flat-mate and not worry about her carrying out the command too literally and snatching one's man away.

George went into the bedroom and started hanging up all the clothes Meredith had thrown on the floor. Most of them were very scruffy and creased and some were downright filthy. The hairbrush by the side of Meredith's bed was thick with hairs and there were clips all over the place.

When Jos came, she was still wearing her leather coat and her hair was dripping again because she'd decided there was still a bit of a wave left in it. Jos pushed the door open with one foot and stood there holding a great greasy newspaper parcel of chips.

'You stink,' George said.

'Come and take them so I can get in,' said Jos.

George walked over and took them and marched through into the kitchen where she threw them in the wastebin with all the dirty cans.

Jos started to hum pleasantly. He sat down in front of the fire, put his feet on the mantelpiece and his hands behind his head.

'You naked underneath that coat?' he asked.

'Stark,' said George.

'Let's 'ave a look then.'

'It's threepence.'

'Too dear, dear.'

George sat down on the rug and started to dry her hair. Jos stopped humming and there was dead silence. When her hair was dry, she went into the kitchen and started peeling vegetables to make some soup and cutting up meat to casserole it. It got hot with the oven on so she chucked her coat on to a chair. Jos jumped up and put it on and turned the collar up then leaned against the door chewing imaginary gum. George refused to laugh, so he took it off again and started helping with the vegetables.

After a bit George said, 'You humouring me?'

Jos hesitated and then said, 'Not exactly. You make me self-conscious.'

'Good God, me?'

'Yeh. I can't stand people hating me.'

'Don't be mad.'

'I'm not. You won't even talk to me.'

'I haven't got anything to say. I'm not like Meredith with all her scintillating chat.'

Jos squirmed and abruptly put down the knife he was using.

'What you making anyway?'

'Don't change the subject. Why don't you say what you're thinking?'

'Which was?'

'Which was how could Meredith, such a pretty gay little girl, share a flat with a great clodhopper like me.'

'Heh, this isn't like you, George,' said Jos.

'No it isn't, is it? Jolly back-slapping hockey stick George.'

'Oh come on, George,' said Jos.

'My name is Georgina.'

'Georgina then. What's eating you? Don't you feel well?'

George threw the carrot she was peeling at him. It hit his spectacles and they fell on to the floor and broke and she sat on the floor beside them and cried. Blindly, Jos squatted down beside her and they both stared at the smashed lenses. Eventually, George stopped crying and started apologizing.

'For God's sake shut up,' Jos said.

They went next door and sat on the sofa. George closed her eyes and concentrated on letting the self-pity wash over her until the taste revolted her.

'This is where I count my blessings,' she said.

'What for?'

'Having two legs and arms and eyes and ears and so on, so it shouldn't matter that I'm as ugly as sin.'

Jos sighed and opened his mouth to speak.

'No, don't say anything. You don't have to pretend I'm not.'

'I wasn't going to. You must know you're just having some sort of seizure or something.'

Having said it, he looked at her. Her mouth was too big and her jaw too heavy and that stupid pony tail didn't help but she wasn't ugly. Her figure was about fifty times better than Meredith's.

'In fact,' he said, 'you just miss being beautiful.'

George smiled and then laughed and finally doubled up, until suddenly she felt Jos's hands on her arms.

'Don't touch me,' she snapped.

'Christ,' said Jos.

He lit a cigarette and thought that if she had been naked under the coat he would have liked it. The trouble was you had to look at her so hard to see she was worth looking at and all the time he couldn't make out whether she deliberately thought and tried to act as though she was ugly.

Meredith came in at ten.

'Kept the chips warm?' she said.

'Yeh. George put them where they'd keep hot.'

'I threw them away,' said George.

'Well I hope you've got something else,' said Meredith and sat on Jos's knee where she kissed and cuddled him until George's soup and casseroled steak were ready and on the table.

When they were finished George said, 'I'm going out.'

'Good,' said Meredith.

'Where?' said Jos.'

'Home.'

'Are you sure you want to? I mean, you're not going because of us or anything?' he said anxiously.

'For God's sake, don't stop her,' said Meredith.

George left and they went to bed, or, at least, into the bedroom. Jos decided he didn't really like Meredith and he didn't know why he was there. He took his tie off and his shoes and sat on the end of the bed thinking what a little bitch she was and how good old George was worth ten of her. He realized 'good old George' wasn't the way to think of her, and told himself to forget the leather coat and imagine a naked girl called Georgina. He vowed to call her Georgina from then on. He lay back and watched Meredith taking her stockings off. She had very hairy legs.

'Why don't you shave your legs?' he said.

'Why should I? They're natural.'

Jos smiled. She might have a moustache when she was older.

'What you smirking at?'

'I was just looking at the thin line of hair on your upper lip and wondering if you ought to have it electrically treated before it's too late.'

Because she was pretty and sought-after she just laughed. Jos watched with satisfaction what she thought were her sexy little ways, such as sliding out of her underslip by pulling the straps down instead of pulling the whole thing over her head. She was the most terrible exhibitionist.

'Meredith,' he said.

'What?'

'How many times have you slept with me?'

'Approx.?'

'Yeh.'

'Oh, six months on an average three times a week makes it seventy-two times. Heh, that's pretty impressive. I've never slept that much with anyone else, bet you.'

'Why do we go on when we don't even like each other all that much?'

'Because we're sexy and like it.'

She'd finished undressing.

'Your toes are dirty,' he said.

She slapped his face, amiably, but hard, and then they made their usual tigerish love.

Meredith slept and Jos lay awake. He'd met her in the orchestra when he took over the double bass for a two months spell while his friend, whose job it was, went into hospital for a stomach operation. She played one of the second violins. She looked a dream with her wild mass of dark hair and her eyes closed in the delicate pale face. She played as if possessed. The entire male section of the orchestra was at her feet either musically, or sexually, or both, even though most of them knew she was a callous, cruel flirt. She'd slept around since she was seventeen and not a single one of the favoured knew what went on in her arrogant little head.

At first, Jos remembered, he'd wanted to marry her, until after he'd known her about three weeks, when he decided nothing could be worse. She was so selfish it made his very straight hair curl with disgust. He'd tried reforming her but she resisted passionately, and now he just went on having this one-sided affair and satisfied his conscience by warning her repeatedly that any day now he would go off and leave her. She said she'd probably have gone first. Lately, he'd kept worrying about her having a baby. If they'd slept together seventy-two times, though, she must be sterile. He was sure he'd be crazy with worry if he was her. He would look after himself. The subject just didn't interest Meredith.

There was a rehearsal for the whole orchestra the next morning so Jos took Meredith down, then went for a walk along the river by himself. He had about five shillings to his name. There was a bitter east wind scudding along the river banks and grey clouds hung low and greedy over the Festival Hall. He started to walk down towards Westminster Bridge, holding himself rigid with cold and unable to relax inside his duffle coat. When he got there he stood at the bus stop and wondered whether it was worth going home if he was going to turn up for Todd's party date. He'd said he would play though he hated one night stands. Todd would get paid, then share out the money about next Christmas, which did him a lot of good. Another few weeks of hanging on like this and then he'd have to go back to the bank, big joke.

The party was, Todd said, a posh do. It was in Mayfair and given by the usual business tycoon with too much money and no taste. His name was James Leamington and it was a party for a particular reason so they had to practise a nauseating birthday tune. When they got there, they were shown into a large, gaudy room and hardly had time to unpack their instruments and get going before the usual types rolled up.

Jos played mechanically, gazing aimlessly at the hordes around him, all twisting like nothing on this earth. There were big mirrors all round the room and he didn't know how they could bear to watch themselves making such a bloody awful exhibition. There was one statuesque dame in particular, with an admiring throng all round, who made him sweat with embarrassment just to watch. She had a good sense of rhythm but she was overdoing it.

When George came across and spoke to him, Jos felt furious.

'Enjoy yourself?' he whispered fiercely.

'Not 'arf mate,' she said brightly.

'What are you doing here?'

'Entertaining, same as you, only my services are free and more appreciated.'

She went off as suddenly as she'd come and was instantly claimed by a fat, middle-aged man who ushered her eagerly into his circle.

'Georgy-porgy's going to sing for us,' he said.

George sang 'I'm a whole lot of woman', mimicking and clowning as she went, until the whole room was shrieking with laughter. James beamed and ordered her to give an encore, and when she'd finished took her off for a drink.

'You're the best entertainment in town, George,' he said, 'you should do it professionally.'

'Ta I'm sure,' said George, rolling her eyes and simpering.

'You make me laugh till I cry,' said James. 'Here, have another.' She took it. 'Give me a kiss, darling,' he said, 'just to show me you still love your Uncle Jimsy-Wimsy.'

George swallowed her rising hysteria and kissed him. She'd been doing it, after all, since she was old enough to reach his great fat lips when he bent down over her pram. But the pattern was changing. The lips lingered now and the eyes leered. He was very drunk.

'Come on, George,' he said, 'it's hot in here.'

She put her glass down and followed him. He'd make her sing some stupid song just for him, then when she'd made a thorough fool of herself he'd say she was wonderful.

He took her to his sitting room.

'What shall I sing?' she said brightly.

'Do you love your old uncle, Georgy?'

'Of course. Passionately. Isn't he the one man who's crazy about me?' said George, wondering why the sarcasm never penetrated.

'That's right. I've done a lot for you, George, and I'll do a lot more. Give me a kiss.'

George dutifully pecked at him. He usually stood still and let her peck, but now he seized her and kissed her full on the mouth. His hands wandered up and down her body until her laugh sent them swiftly back to his sides.

'What are you laughing at?' he said, panting.

'It's so lovely,' said George. She waltzed round him, spreading out her arms. 'What more could a girl want than a devoted uncle who adores encouraging her to make an absolute idiot of herself and then declares himself passionately. It just makes me feel so happy, Jimsy-Wimsy, to know I haven't been reared in vain. No, I've been specially designed to satisfy the most fussy of perverts.'

James struggled not to strike her. Shakily, he mopped his lips with his handkerchief and cursed himself for touching her. He wanted her very much. He always had, ever since he had realized no one else saw how desirable she really was. The more he made her act the fool, and saw other people thinking what an oaf she was, the more he secretly hugged his possession of her to himself. He wanted her to be utterly rejected before he took her completely for his own. He'd tried too soon, he'd lost his sense of timing.

'We'll say no more,' he said pompously. George's laughter infuriated him. 'Stop laughing like that. You're being a very silly little girl.'

'Will you smack me?' lisped George.

Jos saw them go out and come back. He saw how all the women looked pityingly at her and wondered how she'd managed to get herself up to look like an obscenely over-developed twelve year old. He was angry with her. She looked stupid. She had a long row of beads which she swung from side to side like a ruddy pendulum, and a cigarette holder which she stuck between her teeth and made faces round. When she saw him looking at her she shouted 'Coo-ee' and waved like a half-wit so that he frowned with embarrassment. He noticed her eyes were very bright and her cheeks flushed, as though she was having the time of her life. He remembered he didn't know anything about her, so maybe she was.

Chapter Two

George could have hugged them. She was passionate about her youngest class. There were ten of them, all around seven years of age, and they came to her for a dancing lesson twice a week, from their crummy private school round the corner. Each of them had some adorable trait that made her want to pick them up and kiss them.

She pranced into her music room, singing and conducting herself as she went. Then she sat down at the piano, and played a gay tune and whistled at the same time, until the first small face appeared round the door.

'Come in, come into my parlour,' she shouted.

The face broke into a giggle, and disappeared.

'All you flies out there,' she called, 'you've got to come in as though you were all caught up in a web. I'm the spider and I'm playing spidery music.'

One after the other they writhed and crept into the room, each a fly dying a thousand deaths. George burst out laughing and played the music faster and faster, then leapt at them from behind the piano, and they were all caught in her arms. Next, they were machines and clanked their way round her, making whirring noises, until they ran out of oil and broke down. Lastly, they were flecks of dust floating around in the sunshine, which George enjoyed best of all, until she caught sight of the stupid fool in the mirror that was herself. I'm daft, she thought. Crackers. They must be killing themselves laughing at me. She looked at them carefully, but they weren't laughing. They were deadly serious, and they didn't see her for what she was at all.

She showed herself being a machine to Meredith when she went home.

'Look,' she said, standing on one leg, and moving the other up and down like a piston. 'I'm a machine.'

'You're bloody well telling me,' said Meredith.

'No, really. Listen.' She ground her teeth convincingly and rotated her head. 'Don't you think it's good?'

'Marvellous.'

'Do you want to see me being a bit of fairy dust?'

'No.'

'You're rotten. Whackso, jolly jinks, rotten.'

'Are we going out?'

'Why – isn't Jos coming?'

'No. He's playing at a party.'

'Oh – I saw him last night.'

'Where?'

'James's Boozy Binge for Beat-up Bores.'

'What were you doing there?'

'Star of honour. I swung naked on a flying trapeze, while Jos balanced a rubber ball on his knees. Hey – that rhymes.' She started singing the two lines over and over again and then suddenly stopped. 'Of a Sat-di, I dine out, meself. What do you do of a Sat-di?' She started laughing again.

'What's so funny about that?' said Meredith.

'The "of" bit.'

'That's not funny. Queen Victoria used it.'

'That makes it funnier. It's like "to my mind".'

'Everyone says that.'

'I know.'

They went off down the stairs and were nearly at the bottom when George said, 'Hey, what about Pegs?'

'Christ,' said Meredith.

'Aw, come on. Let's ask her.'

She thumped on Peg's door and then, when it opened, flattened herself against the wall. Peg stood there, large and fat with her permanently quizzical expression mixed up with a grin.

'I know who it is,' she announced, her face red and beaming, 'it's Georgina Parkin, so stop messing about.'

27

'Actually, madam, it's a private detective. I've reason to believe this is a house of ill repute and you're the ill reputed.'

'Don't muck about,' said Peg, guffawing, and then folding her short fat arms under the large shelf of her bust.

'Very well,' rapped George, 'I must ask you point blank, since you've forced things to a head, to accompany me to the Station where we'll have a large plate of spaghetti Fred.'

'When you two are finished,' said Meredith.

They walked briskly down the road towards Fred's Caf.

'O.K., Snowy,' whispered George, 'ready to shoot.'

'Bang bang,' said Peg.

'You got him. Behind this boulder, quick – there's no time to lose.'

She pulled the protesting Peg into the doorway of a chemist's. Meredith sighed and walked on disdainfully.

'See that man?' said George. 'We've got to trail him. We've just got to, whatever the risk. If he makes a break for it, you take the left and I'll take the right. Good luck, Snowy.'

At Fred's they all ordered spaghetti and George smoked while it came.

'Disgusting,' said Peg, frowning at the same time as she laughed, to show that she meant it.

George sighed, and stubbed it out.

'You're a hard woman, Peg Feather,' she said, 'you have your vices but you won't let me have mine.'

'I haven't got any vices.'

'Oh no – not much. We all know about her, don't we Meredith? Drinking, drugs and men. I can tell you, my dear Peg, that if it wasn't for us guarding your secret so closely it would have all been up with you long ago, my word yes. Wouldn't it Meredith?'

Meredith ate in silence. She didn't know which was worse: George jolly or George gloomy. She laughed in spite of herself once or twice, but mainly she just ate and looked cynically at the pair of them. *She* was sorry for Peg too, who wouldn't be, but she thought it unhealthy for George to go around with her too much. She used her as a sort of 'Count your blessings' talisman which didn't do Peg any good either.

'Tomorrow is Sunday,' said George, 'thank God.'

'Why?' said Peg.

'Because I don't have to work. Fancy asking that. Don't you live for Sundays?'

'Nope.'

'Well, you have Saturday off too, and all those holidays.'

'Don't like Saturdays either or holidays,' Peg was still laughing and frowning at the same time to such a mixed up extent that Meredith felt all churned up inside.

'Why not?' said George. 'Come on, Peg Feather, why not, eh?'

'Boring.'

'Don't you do anything?'

'Nope.'

'Don't you go to the pictures?'

'Nope.'

'My God, how do you live? Read then?'

'Don't like reading.'

'Go for walks?'

'Not by myself.'

George began to sweat with desperation. Please, please, she prayed, don't let her be so miserable. I couldn't bear it.

'A likely story,' she said, gaily. 'Out on the tiles every night, Peg Feather, and trying to kid on you don't do anything.'

Before Peg could insist, she ordered some coffee and gave a spirited imitation of James kissing her the night before. Even Meredith laughed. Peg couldn't stop, and eventually braced herself with both arms against the wall.

'Heh,' said George, 'look at Peg Feather's arms.'

'One's wonky,' said Meredith.

'Keep still,' said George, 'don't move until I get the doctor.'

'Don't be daft,' said Peg, delightedly, 'you can feel if you like. Broke one of them.' They both felt the bony knob above one elbow while Peg proudly related the story that went with it.

'I've got to go,' said Meredith.

'Where? I thought Jos was at a party?' said George, in surprise.

'He is. I'm not going with Jos. Cheerio.'

Hurt, George groped for another cigarette. Meredith could

have told her earlier. It didn't matter, but she could have bloody well have told her, instead of leading her on to think they were going to spend the evening together.

There was no alternative. She had to ask Peg back for coffee. Dreading it, she invited her and they walked back, this time without any games, and at a much slower pace. George dried up. She tried hard to think of something inane to say, or do, to stem the flood of moans that Peg was bound to let go when they were alone. As she felt her own reluctance to play father confessor, it struck her that maybe people felt like that when *she* was moody. But they could never feel as sorry for her as she felt for Peg.

They went past Peg's door and up to George's flat. George made some coffee and put a very noisy record on. Even under cover of that, there was an uncompanionable silence.

'Where's Meredith gone?' Peg said.

'With some fella I expect.'

'Wish we could get boys as easily as she does,' said Peg, still giggling through her air of gloom, 'but who'd have us?'

'Who indeed?' murmured George, horrified. She had an almost painful urge to go and look at herself in the mirror. Instead, she furtively looked at Peg. She was enormous – not just fat, but enormous so there must be something wrong with her glands. Her large round face was red and shiny and her small nose was turned fiercely up so that you looked straight into her nostrils, which luckily she kept very clean. This unfortunate nose left permanently in view the top row of her teeth, which were very small, and widely spaced, and set in a broad gum so that there was much more gum than teeth. Her hair was thin and black, scraped back into a bunch of scrawny curls at the back. She sat like a farm yacker, knees well apart, and had a habit of punching herself on her fat thighs with her clenched fist as though chastising herself.

George smiled.

'What are you laughing at?' said Peg, and then without waiting for a reply, 'You're always laughing at me.'

George flushed crimson.

'I can't help it,' she said, 'you're so sort of jolly. You cheer me up.'

'I'm not jolly. I suppose you think I'm fat and happy?' said Peg.

'No, I don't think that,' said George, 'but I wish you were.'

Peg's face had lost its grin. It was bare and mean. She'd wanted George to say she wasn't fat. It wouldn't have mattered that it was a lie. She didn't care how many lies people told if it made her feel better, and somehow it always did.

'I'm going,' she said, sulkily, 'thanks for the coffee.'

'That's all right,' said George, unhappily, 'see you.'

The minute Peg had waddled off she flew to the mirror. She wasn't fat, she hadn't any disfiguring features, in fact if she did something with her hair and didn't wear such daft clothes she'd be quite something. That is, compared with Peg, and always remembering that nothing *could* be done with her hair and any other sort of clothes looked silly on her.

The bell rang and she raised her eyebrows at her reflection. She took her glasses off as she went to answer and consciously practised a casual smile. It was James.

'Hello Georgy-Porgy,' he said, stepping in before she'd recovered. 'I thought I'd come round and see how my little girl was getting on.'

He had a large box of chocolates in one hand. George automatically took them and put them on the table. He went across and stood with his back to the fire.

'I'm forty-nine,' he said.

'Is that all?' said George, absentmindedly.

'That's all. Forty-nine. I was twenty-two, and just married myself, when you were born. Your father was thirty and your mother was twenty-four. If it hadn't been for me they would never have been able to get married. Your father was an out-of-work mechanic when I met him and I remember him saying, when I offered him a job as my valet, that he was afraid I might be very angry if he said he wanted to get married. I said all the better because I wanted a cook and housekeeper too. I was setting up house myself. We used to talk about the children we would have. You might not believe that, but we did. I never had any, and Ted only had you. I was determined, Georgy, to give you everything I'd have given a daughter of my own. I've always thought of you as a daughter. But you're not, and it's only now that I thank God for it.'

'Why?' said George, blandly.

'Because then I couldn't do what I'm going to do.'

George looked at him, cautiously. It wasn't very long since she'd been scared stiff of him. Her father had successfully dinned into her that without James their mouths would be empty and the roof taken off their heads. She shook in case she did something wrong, and looked at her mother with terror when she muttered that might be a good thing. When she was at school, the sight of James's Rolls meant more to her than anything else and if she did something specially good she knew James's smile of approval instantly earned a hundred more from her cipher of a father. And yet, in spite of the education and the constant visits and gifts, he'd never really shown much interest in her. He'd never talked to her, beyond the teasing remark or grunt of agreement. She didn't know a thing about him, except that he was kind, busy, rich and occasionally bad-tempered. Once, he'd been the tall, strange uncle who was always magnificent and aloof; now, he was the large, benevolent socialite whose sense of humour was limited and sense of power overgrown. He rather repelled her.

She tried to look at him as though she'd never seen him before, which wasn't impossible because she'd always been too much in awe of him, cr lately too intent on getting away, to really stare.

If her father was a mere eight years older than him then James had worn well. He was in his prime, like a slab of red steak. His hair was still thick and black, his face hardly lined at all, though the bags under his eyes told another tale. He was definitely developing a paunch, but he carried it high up, the way some women do their babies, and it gave him a presence he wouldn't otherwise have had. Usually, he beamed expansively on anybody and everybody, but tonight his face was grave, and therefore more likeable.

'What was that?' she said.

'Make you an offer.'

'What for? You've already given me so much and you know I don't want anything more. I thought I'd explained.'

'I don't mean that,' said James, impatiently. 'I've got over you moving out and living on that damn dancing class or whatever you call it. It's nothing to do with money.'

George thought, with relief, that that was a change. She waited, but James seemed to want her to guess. She couldn't think of anything.

'I don't know,' she said, slowly, 'unless you want to engage me as your clown.'

'I want you to be my mistress,' said James, abruptly. 'I've been thinking about it for a long time and I think it would work very well. What I propose is an agreement whereby either one of the contracting parties is free to opt out at any time, without notice, during a six months' initial period, and then at a month's notice thereafter. I'll bear all the expense, of course, and undertake the formal adoption of any children. We'll keep it secret, though Nell knows I've done this before, and she'd be a fool to object. Of course, we've nothing to worry about as far as your parents are concerned. I've got the draft of a contract here. Would you like to look at it?'

She was looking a bit stunned, but then he'd expected that, poor girl. She went around looking such a sight that she couldn't have imagined he'd overlook the glasses and big chin, and that anyway beauty didn't interest him very much. Nell was beautiful and marrying her had been about his one mistake in life. George was intelligent and knew how to enjoy herself: those were the things that mattered.

'You're not offended because I've made it sound too business-like, are you?' he said, when she said nothing after he'd waited patiently for some time, 'because believe me, it's always the best way.'

'I'm sure it is,' murmured George. 'I mean, I might slip my mooring and sail away. You make me sound like a ship.'

'I thought you'd prefer that. I can be romantic as you like, given half a chance.'

As if to substantiate this, he at last removed his bulk from in front of the fire and tentatively touched her arm.

'That's nice,' said George.

'I can do better than that,' said James, and eagerly brought both arms round her. George shook him off.

'I meant the warmth from the fire actually. You've been blocking it all from me.'

'Aren't you going to say yes or no?'

'Yes or no,' said George, and giggled.

James swore. 'You fool about too much,' he said.

'What will you do, Sir King, if I say no?' she asked. 'Burn mine humble dad at the stake?'

'He won't know anything about it either way. We'll just forget about it and go on as before. I hardly ever see you these days, and I don't support you any more, so I don't see that it would cause any embarrassment.'

'I'm a virgin,' George said.

'Think I didn't know that?'

'Well, wouldn't you feel mean seducing a young innocent like me then leaving me as poor, shoddy, second-hand goods for life?'

'No,' said James, 'it would do you good.'

George let him kiss her, and tested all her reactions carefully. He smelt of cigars and shaving lotion which was very pleasant. His kiss, unlike the fiasco of the night before, was firm and dry, and she was startled to find his hands on her breasts excited her. It was really amazing.

'The thing is,' she said carefully, 'that it's not true what they say.'

'What do they say.'

'That a woman has to be roused by someone before she has any sexual awakening, where a man would feel it on a desert island. I've felt it for years, in an absolute vacuum and it doesn't need anyone to rouse me. I'm just ripe for plucking, daddy-o.'

'That's what I think too,' said James.

George giggled again. 'Do you know,' she said, 'I used to get

34

myself into an absolute passion when I was about twelve imagining myself stripping in front of men. I just couldn't wait for sex. I still can't. I can imagine exactly what it will be like. Can't you?'

'Er – yes,' said James.

'Oh I forgot, of course you can. It would be rather funny if you couldn't, wouldn't it.'

To James' annoyance, her giggles got out of control and she lay back on the sofa, killing herself laughing. He got up and went back to his place in front of the fire and lit a cigar, putting the contract back in his wallet pocket.

'I can see it's no good talking to you in this mood,' he said pompously. 'What you're indulging in now isn't laughter, it's silliness. Now sober up, Georgy,' he added in a softer tone, 'and give me some idea of what your answer's going to be.'

The doorbell rang. 'Twice in one evening,' said George. 'This must be a record.'

'Don't answer it,' said James.

'Why ever not?'

'Because we're in the middle of something important.'

She came back with Jos.

'Jos,' she said, 'this is my uncle, Mr Leamington.'

'How do you do sir,' said Jos stiffly.

'And Uncle Jim, this is Jos. He plays the double bass. He played it at your party last night, actually.'

'Oh, did he?' said James, disturbed. She'd kept stressing the uncle bit, and anyway he hadn't known she had any boyfriends. Even one weedy, bespectacled musician made a difference.

'How long have you known George?' he asked.

'Well, it's really Meredith I know,' said Jos.

'Who's Meredith?'

'The girl who shares this flat with me,' said George.

James beamed. Everything was quite clear. He decided he'd better go, all the same.

'I'll be waiting to hear from you George,' he said, when he got to the door. 'The sooner the better, either way.'

'Bastard,' said George, as she came back into the room.

'Him or me?' said Jos.

'You. It wouldn't have cost you much to let him think you were my boyfriend.'

'How was I to know you wanted me to?'

'Oh, never mind. Meredith isn't in. I thought you were playing at a party?'

'It was cancelled. I thought she might just have decided to stay in. Do you know where she's gone?'

'No.'

George felt remote from Jos instead of very aware of him, as she usually did. She sat down on the sofa, and folding her arms, stared at the picture above the mantelpiece. It was terrible to think that James was the only man interested in her. She might never have another offer, never be loved or anything. She actually felt tempted. She wanted sex so badly, she told herself, any man would do, and she'd quite enjoyed his kiss, so why be ashamed to admit it?

Vaguely, she was aware that Jos was still standing. She drew her eyes from the picture and focused on him. He looked depressed.

'What's wrong?' she said. 'Are you hurt that Meredith's gone out?'

'Don't be bloody silly. I know I'm only one among many for her, and, for that matter, so is Meredith for me.'

'Sorry. I forgot the pair of you just can't find time to fit in all your admirers.'

'Aw, shut up. It makes me sick, that sort of talk.'

George obediently shut up.

'It's my job,' said Jos, eventually, 'or my lack of one. Another couple of weeks and I'll have to go back to working in a bloody bank. I can't get a permanent job and temporary ones are badly paid, when you think how long there is between them.'

'Does money matter?'

'Oh Christ!'

'I mean, don't you have enough to scrape by on?'

'I'm twenty-eight. I can't always go on scraping. I might want to get married one day.'

'What does Meredith think?'

'As you know, Meredith doesn't care.'

'I think you ought to stick to music, somehow. Have you tried every single orchestra there is?'

'There aren't that many in London.'

'Well, outside London.'

'Hell, I couldn't go to Manchester or somewhere like that.'

'Why not? If you really wanted to play for a living, and a job came up there, it shouldn't matter what sort of place it is.'

'It shouldn't, but it does.'

'Why?'

'Music's second. Enjoying myself is first, and I couldn't enjoy myself there. Everything's dead after six and entertainment-wise there's nothing at all outside London. Satisfied?'

'I'm jealous.'

'Of what?'

'All this enjoying you do. I would never have imagined, looking at you now, that life was just a ball.'

Jos smiled and began to walk round the room. George stayed where she was.

'I didn't know he was your uncle.'

'He isn't. My father works for him and he's a sort of self-imposed fairy godfather.' She started to giggle, as she had done when James was there. Jos came and sat beside her.

'That,' he said, 'does my old, enjoying heart good. Although Fairy James didn't look a very laughable prospect to me. What was he doing here, anyway?'

'He had a proposition to make.'

'Evil?'

'Naturally. He wants me to be his mistress and set up house with him and rear his children, being as 'ow he is passionate with love for me.'

'No wonder he looked a bit blue when I came in. Did I interrupt your outraged reply?'

37

'There wasn't one.'

'You didn't agree, for God's sake?'

'I didn't have time to do anything except giggle like this.'

'When will you tell him?'

'When I've made my mind up.'

Jos stared, and then turned away with what was obviously intended to be a look of disgust. George flushed angrily. He had no right to condemn anything she might do. There was nothing more disgusting in James's proposed alliance with her than there was in his with Meredith. Maybe he merely found it physically, pictorially disgusting because James was big and fat, and she was ugly.

'I hope you're kidding,' Jos said.

'It's nothing to do with you,' said George, sharply.

'Course it has. Nobody could stand by and watch that happen.'

'What makes you think you're so virtuous?'

'I'm not. But at least I lust where I sleep and love where I love. You wouldn't be doing either. What would you get out of it?'

'A man of my own.'

'You must be hard up,' said Jos, without thinking.

'I am. Desperate, that's me. Twenty-seven and never been asked out by a fella, let alone kissed. Pathetic, isn't it?' said George brightly.

Jos sighed. He decided he would go because in a minute the self-pitying sobs would break out, and after that the remorse, which was far worse. He turned his coat collar up and put his hands in his pockets. She went on smiling vivaciously at that damn picture.

'Come on,' he said, suddenly, 'let's go.'

'Where?' said George, startled.

'I haven't an idea. Just out of this dump for a start.'

'If you're just asking me because of what I said a minute ago, you needn't bother.'

'No, I needn't, and yet, I am asking you.' He strode out and she followed.

Jos didn't think where he was going, mainly because in his experience he'd never had to decide. Meredith and all his other sleeping partners usually let him know what they wanted to do and they accordingly did it. It wasn't a case of being weak-willed, as he usually chose his girls because they liked doing what he did. That selection seemed limited as he walked down the road with George. Usually, if he and Meredith went for a meal, it was to stoke themselves up before bed; if they went to a club of some kind, and danced, it was a limbering up process before the real business of the evening began. Even a picture would be carefully chosen to act as an aphrodisiac. Without the end product, none of these pastimes was attractive.

He kept walking while he thought, trying to look as though he knew why they were crossing from one corner to another. He couldn't go to bed with George. It wasn't that she was all that repulsive because he'd already decided that she wasn't, but she'd talk so damn much and be analysing his motives and her own reactions all the time. One thing Meredith and her kind had in their favour was that they knew what bed was for, and didn't mess up the process with a lot of tiring monologues. It seemed a shame that James would be the first to have her though, sheer waste. Jos felt it might almost be worth all the soul-searching and interrogation that would follow, just to queer his pitch.

He decided a drink was an essential prelude to any sort of action, so he turned into a bar, and George followed. She had a half pint of bitter, which he thought rather unnecessary, and he had a whisky. He was at a terrible loss for anything to say. He didn't do much talking with his women, not because he thought they couldn't make intelligent conversation, but because he thought all conversation was pretty futile anyway. It made him laugh till he almost kicked himself when he heard couples in restaurants and places having spirited repartee sessions. The only ones he respected were the ones who kept stone-silent.

'How long have you worked in a bank?' said George. He looked at her warily, in case she was going to be all gay and tra-la.

'From when I was sixteen to last June. That made it eleven years and ten months.'

'Why did you start work there in the first place?'

'Please teacher, because I had to earn my living and that was the only thing the lousy Youth Employment Officer had in his little book.'

'What did you do all those eleven years? It must have been very boring,' said George.

Jos closed his eyes. It wasn't true that all his girls had been like Meredith. Once, a little debbie type, all do-gooding, had picked him up when he played at her party and asked the same inane questions in her pretty, polite voice.

'You don't have to do anything,' he said, 'you just work. It isn't very painful. Millions do it, so don't ask me as though I'd been a convict or something.'

'I wish my father did that,' said George.

'What's he do, anyway?'

'He's a valet. He doesn't do very much at all except look after James. The uncle you saw.'

'Good luck to him,' said Jos.

'I think it's degrading,' said George.

Jos smiled. 'You'd make a good suburban housewife,' he said. She flushed and he felt sorry. She was always making him feel apologetic.

They didn't talk any more and he had to think of somewhere to go. He made for the jazz club where he sometimes played, if he was lucky, when the resident double bass player was ill. Once he'd got in he felt scared in case George would make a fool of herself the way she had done at that party. She might do some sort of extravagant twist or something. But she seemed to have gone quiet and docile, perhaps sulking or maybe this was her martyred attitude. They danced. There wasn't much room, so, except for a few couples on the fringe, no one was twisting, they were just moving round vaguely in time to the music. George was the same height as he was and she had an excellent sense of time. They danced well together and he was relieved that at least one thing wasn't an ordeal.

'You're a good dancer,' he said.

'So I should be. I teach it.'

He was surprised, and then felt guilty again because he'd never once asked what she did or even wondered.

'What do you teach? Kids?'

'Kids.'

'Do you like it?'

'Yes.'

He felt irrationally pleased and automatically relaxed. They left the club and he took her for an Italian meal, then they went for a walk along the river, which was a habit of his. He didn't bother asking her whether she wanted to or not. He did.

They got home about two in the morning. Meredith wasn't home.

'I'm sorry Meredith isn't back yet,' said George as she brought him some coffee.

'No one mentioned Meredith,' he said. He noticed she was hanging his coat up on a hanger. Eventually, she came and sat beside him.

'Thank you for the evening.'

'A pleasure, obviously.'

He put the coffee down and, rather cruelly, turned her face towards his. It was painfully there what she wanted. He could almost hear her heart thudding and hormones racing. He felt amused, but didn't dare smile. It was absolutely impossible not to tantalize her. He picked the coffee up again and watched her swallow hard. When he'd finished it, he got up and took it through into the kitchen, then came back and took his jacket off before he sat down again. He kissed her very lightly on the lips and nearly exploded at the violence of the tremor which swept through her. He put his arms round her and caressed her and she responded as though she'd been saving up for it since she was born.

Jos felt weak and suddenly fed up. It wouldn't take much effort to lay her and he would enjoy it. But God, the aftermath. He was a casual, easy going sort of bloke. He couldn't take it, especially from someone he didn't give a damn about. That was the snag – he did actually feel responsible for her. It was the danger signal. It was in his own interests not to be a bastard, just for half an hour's enjoyment.

Regretfully, because by now he felt quite amorous and it was a shame to have got her so worked up, he loosened his hold and sat up.

'Sorry about that,' he said.

'Why?' said George. 'I like it. What are you stopping for?'

He was silent.

'I know I'm not pretty like Meredith,' she said.

'Oh Christ,' he said, 'that's why – I can't stand all this "I'm-so-humble" stuff. After we'd been to bed it would be one long whine.'

She burst into tears and fled into the bedroom. He lit a cigarette and stayed where he was. Five minutes later she tore out again with her coat on, and he heard her running down the stairs and slamming the outside door. He sat there, feeling content because he'd done the right thing. When he was about to go, Meredith suddenly appeared. She showed no surprise at finding him there.

'Had a good time?' he said.

'So-so.'

'Didn't lead to bed so can't have been up to much, mate.'

'Exactly.'

They sat smoking for a bit and Jos was glad that he didn't have to turf himself out into the cold night air. Meredith curled up beside him and put her arms round his neck.

'You're very affectionate,' he said.

'I want to talk.'

'Oh no!' Jos groaned.

'Yes. I like you better than any man I've ever had and I'm getting bored with living with George. Maybe I will marry you. We don't fight, we make love divinely and we get along.'

'You must be pregnant,' said Jos.

'Yes.'

For the second time that night he turned a face to scrutinize. All George thought and felt had been on hers. He could see practically nothing in Meredith's.

'Meredith,' he said, slowly, 'there is no point at all in us getting married when I know nothing about you except things I don't like.'

'You sound like my father,' she said.

'Who was your father anyway? Where do you come from?'

'Out of the ground. I'm a pixie. What the hell does it matter? I can't stand all this family stuff. I haven't seen mine for years and I don't intend to. You take me as me.'

'Who's you?'

'Don't start airy-fairy rubbish like that. I don't ask you what you are. I know you're attractive, twenty-eight, a good musician, kind, conceited and good tempered.'

'I don't know that much about you.'

'Do you have to, for God's sake?'

'Yes, for God's sake, if we're going to get married and have this kid.'

'All right then, if there's all this fuss we needn't get married and the kid's easily disposed of. It's only minus seven months old.'

She folded her arms and put her feet up across his knees, then put her tongue out. He didn't laugh. She decided the only good gift she'd got from her parents at birth was detachment. She really was detached. She looked at everything through an inverted glass and was proud that nothing touched her, except perhaps occasional love-making or playing her violin in some concertos, and even then she felt ashamed. Some people thought she was hard, others that she was just stupid. Jos thought she pretended. He sometimes tried to force her, at the climax of her love making, to admit that she loved him and cared about him and passionately wanted to know every detail of his life. She didn't.

He was wrong if he thought the great clue to why she was like she was lay in her past. Her parents were ordinary – ordinary, dull, boring and endlessly caught up in petty speculation and worries. She'd manufactured her own identity, deliberately, not because she'd been hurt or anything so dramatic, but just because she had felt proud to think she could do it. She hadn't stopped when she'd decided to have the baby and marry Jos either. It would be fun to have more things to be detached about. She tried hard to be detached about Jos, but had to admit she did care just a bit what happened to him. She would definitely miss him if he went. Ought she, therefore, for that very reason, to give him up?

'Is it the baby?' said Jos.

'What.'

'That makes you decide you'll marry me. You've always laughed at the very idea.'

'Partly. I just feel like a change. But I've told you – you don't have to. I can easily get rid of the baby. I've no tender feelings about it.'

'I have,' said Jos, gloomily. 'I always knew I would have. I couldn't let you destroy it.'

'Don't be stupid,' said Meredith, tartly. 'I've destroyed two of yours already.'

Jos stared at her. 'When?'

'I've forgotten. You've made me pregnant twice and I've got rid of them, that's all.'

'Why didn't you tell me? Didn't I have a right to know? Weren't they my responsibility as well as yours?' shouted Jos.

He felt furious – tricked and deprived. It was terrible to think his sons and daughters were dead and he never even knew about it. Meredith was laughing. He couldn't understand how she'd done it all on her own, and desperately wanted to know the exact details of the murders.

'You're not killing this one,' he said.

'I will if I want,' chanted Meredith.

'I won't let you.'

'You can't stop me.'

'We'll get married tomorrow.'

'Fine.'

He hurled a cushion at her, in a rage because everything she did was so painstakingly drained of any feeling. He could imagine George in a similar situation, all tears and panic, and then ecstatic at the thought of marriage and motherhood. Meredith wasn't worried, excited, disturbed in any way. He could have said yes, or no, or maybe, and got exactly the same response.

He took hold of her shoulders and shook her hard. Her pretty dark head lolled backwards and forwards, smiling, and then she slapped his face and he slapped hers back and they started fighting in earnest, picking and punching and rolling from the sofa to the floor in an exhilarated huddle. Then they went to bed and Jos reflected that for as long as it lasted this was their natural destiny.

George was going to go home when she left Jos, but half-way there she thought better of it. It was always impossible to get into that house without Ted hearing and coming down and that was the last thing she wanted. There would be questions and scenes and she'd probably end up by being thrown out, or walking out again.

She always seemed to be rushing in tears from places, though each time she vowed that above all she would have self-control. It sounded such a little thing, but her tears came so suddenly and engulfed her before she had time to remember that this was supposed to be what she was putting a stop to. She'd spoiled a lovely evening, which was typical too. She'd thrown herself at Jos when he was only being kind and feeling sorry for her and she'd never be able to face him again. She'd have to move. She'd accept James's revolting offer and see what good a course in masochism would do her.

At first, she thought she would walk all night, but she'd already walked a long way with Jos and she was tired. No one thought big, strapping girls might get tired, but she was. She hadn't enough money for a bed and breakfast place, let alone an hotel, and anyway that would mean more explanations, more words. Uncertainly, she began walking back the way she had come until she found herself in the square again and outside her house. The light was out in the living room so Jos had probably gone. She tiptoed up and very softly opened the door, her heart thumping in case he was still there and she would have to endure the humiliation of running out all over again. He had gone. Sighing, she stopped tiptoeing and walked into the bedroom, where she snapped on the light.

'Put that bloody light off,' said Meredith.

Blindly, George groped for the switch and obeyed.

'That's better. Now get out.'

George stumbled out. She got herself outside the flat and down the first few stairs and felt the tears again but this time cursed herself and held on, dry-eyed. She knocked at Peg Feather's door. She had to do it a few times before Peg emerged, swaddled in a tartan dressing gown bristling with curlers.

'What's the matter? Someone dead?'

Even at that time of night, she had to giggle, in spite of being cross and tired.

'Nearly,' said George. 'Can you put me up for the rest of the night?'

'I've only got my bed. Though it's a double one.'

Wearily, George followed and nodded her head gratefully. Peg was asking the why's and wherefore's and she couldn't be bothered to even answer. She took off her coat and skirt and jumper, and crawled in beside the mammoth winceyetted Peg and thankfully turned onto her side and slept.

Upstairs, Jos tried to work out the significance of George's entry. The sight of them nude and asleep might have been a traumatic experience for her.

'Meredith.' He nudged her hard. 'Hey, I'm worried about George. You don't think she'll do anything silly do you?'

'No. Good night.'

'She's in an upset state.'

'She's always upset. Good night.'

'No, but really – I happen to know that uncle James of hers asked her to be his mistress tonight.'

He waited, but Meredith was asleep. He thought bitterly that any other woman would have leapt out of bed at such a sensational piece of gossip about her best friend. So he slept too, and expected she was right. George had too much homely good sense to be silly and anyway she was a big strong girl who could take care of herself.

Chapter Three

It was a vicious, wet Sunday. By eleven o'clock it hardly seemed light at all, and the grey thickness of the rain clawed imploringly at the window panes. The square was deathly quiet, no traffic, no passers by, it was sealed off. From one corner emerged Peg, with a pack-a-mac over her gaberdine and an umbrella held stiffly and vertically overhead. Like a smudge on a radar screen, she thumped across the square and up the steps to Number Seventeen.

Usually, Peg took a long time cleaning her shoes on the mat and generally employing delaying tactics, especially on Sundays. Church only took up a couple of hours, even though she didn't go to the nearest one and always walked there and back. She left at ten, got back at twelve, made and ate her lunch at one and then the grim business of getting through to evensong began.

But today she had company. It would mean halving her chop down the middle which was an operation of such delicacy that she shuddered at the thought, but it was worth it to have a guest whom she hadn't even invited.

She went into her room and squelched over to the bed still in her wellingtons and pack-a-mac.

'I suppose you'll want lunch?' she said to the curled-up George. 'Good job I always keep a lot of potatoes in to spin things out. What would you have done if I hadn't kept spare potatoes?'

'I hate to think,' said George, fervently.

'You'll have to get up,' said Peg.

George looked up at her swathed and swaddled figure, from whose tank-like sides the rain dripped reluctantly. Tightly fastened over Peg's head was a rain-proof, pixie-hood affair, that strapped in her fat cheeks until her face looked like one large gumboil.

'Good sermon?' said George.

'Don't mock,' said Peg, laughing and frowning. 'It would do you a lot more good to go to church than lie here like this.'

'Why?' teased George.

'Never you mind,' said Peg. 'It would.'

'Aren't you going to take your armour off?' said George. 'You're wetting all your carpet.'

Peg looked down with interest at the splattering of rain drops round her wellingtons. There were two circles – one quite near coming from the bottom of her mac, and the other a good foot away, coming from her shoulders.

'I've made a mess,' she said.

'You have that,' said George, 'go and take your mac off at once, do you hear?'

'Yes, mummy,' giggled Peg, and waddled happily off to do the necessary unveiling.

George went on lying there. The bed was uncompromisingly in the middle of the room. It had a head board and a foot board and Peg kept a large emerald-coloured eiderdown on the top throughout the day and night. She was the only person George knew who had a sideboard and a double wardrobe through choice. The sideboard had three lace mats on top – one in the middle and smaller ones on each of the slightly raised side bits. The wardrobe had a big mirror inset in the door. They were both a dull walnut. She shifted her gaze to the window, partially obscured by lace netting strung on a rod across the bottom half. The curtains were drawn almost to the middle and were a muddy brown colour. The only concession to the new Elizabethan age was a loudly checked easy chair with a vivid yellow cushion perched uncomfortably on one wooden-slatted arm.

The air of the room was heavy and quiet. George stirred in the bed, and the resulting creak ricocheted round the walls. Peg taking off her mac in the kitchen made regular crackling noises punctuated by the heavy breathing and sighs of effort, as her wellington heels stuck on her socks. Eventually, she emerged looking like an enormous caterpillar, and stood in the middle of the room swinging her short arms and giggled.

'Get up,' she said, and advanced menacingly. George felt apprehensive. The large, green clad body was bending over her and trying to tickle her. She rolled over and Peg slapped her bottom, laughing hysterically and clambering on to the bed.

'Don't Peg, please,' said George, abruptly. Peg went on prodding her body with her podgy fingers, moving them up and down in what she imagined was a tickling action. Kicking desperately, George reached the end of the bed and catapulted over it on to the carpet. She got up quickly, but Peg was nearest her clothes.

'Sling those across please,' she begged.

'Shan't,' said Peg. She'd somehow managed the amazing feat of sitting cross legged, so that to George she looked like some immensely threatening Buddha.

George knew she was only joking. It was a joke to tickle her, it meant nothing, but she was frightened, unreasonably. She didn't want Peg to touch her so closely as though she were some kind of plaything, and she didn't want Peg to see how she felt.

She walked towards the door in her pants and bra.

'Where you going?' said Peg.

'Upstairs to get my clothes. Never mind about lunch.'

'You can have them,' said Peg anxiously. 'Here.' She thrust the skirt and sweater over in a bundle.

George caught them and slipped into them. 'Thanks for having me,' she said, 'I'll see you soon.' She was out of the door before Peg's face had crumbled.

She was inside the door of her flat before she remembered about Jos, and then it was too late because Meredith had heard her.

'George – bring us some coffee.'

Automatically, George went into the kitchen and prepared the percolator. She stood over it while it bubbled, then set a tray with sugar and milk and two cups. When the coffee was almost ready, she made some toast, and carrying it all into the bedroom, put it down just inside the door and left.

'I can't bloody well reach from here,' yelled Meredith. 'Bring it to the bedside, you idiot.'

George stayed where she was in the kitchen. She heard Meredith swear and try to persuade Jos to get up. He appeared asleep. There was a thud as Meredith's feet hit the floor. George waited for her to pick the tray up and curse again, but instead she heard a groan and as she got up she saw Meredith staggering into the bathroom. She reached her just as she vomited into the lavatory. The sound, wretched and painful, brought Jos to the door. They both stood anxiously watching as Meredith went on being sick.

Eventually, she stopped. Her slight body was bent double as though in worship and the thin strands of black hair on the nape of her neck clung in intricate patterns to the perspiration around it. George knelt beside her.

'You look terrible,' she said.

'Thanks.'

'I've never known you be sick.'

Meredith groaned with fury. 'Will you shut up and stop gaping,' she said. 'Why don't you do something useful?'

'Like what?' said Jos, helplessly.

'Go away!' yelled Meredith.

Unhappily, Jos wandered off, while George mopped up the mess, and then helped Meredith back into the bedroom. She gave her some coffee, and watched as the pallor faded.

'You'd better see a doctor,' said George, reprovingly, 'unless it's just because you got drunk last night.'

'I am never sick after I've been drunk as you well know,' said Meredith sharply, 'and anyway I wasn't drunk.'

'Maybe you've got a bug,' said George, helpfully.

Meredith smiled. 'That's a good name for it – the Bug.' She sat up, and lit a cigarette. George became uncomfortably aware of Jos and the night before. She tried to concentrate on Meredith, who was looking perfectly normal again. She'd pulled on a white shift-like garment when she got up, and looked like a small, pretty girl who'd just had her tonsils out.

'I wonder what made you sick?' said George, for something to say.

'My dear child,' said Meredith, 'have you never heard of early morning sickness in pregnancy? Though God knows why I should get it. I just bloody well hope it doesn't happen again or I won't go through with the blasted business.'

George sat very still on the edge of the bed. Jos and Meredith both watched her closely.

'What day is it?' asked Meredith.

'Sunday,' said George, dully.

'Can you get married on Sundays?'

'No. At least, I don't think so. It maybe depends on whether you get married in church or a register office. If you were a Jew it would be a help.'

'Are you a Jew?' Meredith said to Jos.

'No. Are you?'

'I don't think so. When shall we get married then? Tomorrow? No, not a Monday.'

'I'll have to get a licence,' Jos said.

'Why! I'm not a dog,' said Meredith.

'Where are we going to live?' asked Jos.

'Where do you think? Here of course.'

'Don't be stupid,' Jos said, angrily, miserably aware that George had flushed crimson.

'Well, where do you suggest? I've never been to wherever you live. Where do you live anyway? Can we go there?'

'No,' said Jos. 'I live in a lousy bed-sitting room in Earls Court.'

'My God,' said Meredith. 'And you turn your nose up at this. George's flat is about the only nice one I know.'

'Exactly,' said Jos, 'it's George's flat. Hasn't it occurred to you that she definitely won't want a married couple and baby sharing her two rooms k and b? Where do you expect her to sleep, you selfish bitch?'

'On that extremely comfortable divan in the sitting room,' said Meredith. 'There's absolutely nothing wrong with it, is there George?'

'Nothing at all,' said George, quietly.

She wanted to ask Meredith why she wasn't getting rid of this baby like all the others. As far as she knew, Meredith had disposed of four altogether, in spite of George's passionate pleas for her not to. She only knew because the last twice Meredith had borrowed £20 from her. When George had tried to refuse, and force her to have the baby, Meredith had said that if she couldn't get the money to have it done properly she'd get some dirty old woman to do it with a pair of knitting-needles. So George had given in, swearing it was the last time.

Perhaps it was to keep Jos, but Meredith had never wanted to keep anyone as she had repeatedly told George. And anyway, she could probably have done that without getting herself pregnant. It was more likely just a whim she had, as egoistic and unthinking as all her whims. George tried to despise her, but it was hard. Meredith was so small and pale and cold.

'I'm getting up,' said Meredith. She stood up and took the shift off. George blushed furiously.

'Must you?' said Jos.

'What? Good God, you've both seen me naked enough times.' She got dressed as slowly and as provocatively as possible.

'What time's lunch, George?'

'I'm going home,' George said.

'That's a bloody dirty trick,' said Meredith, angrily. 'What do you expect me to do?'

'I'm sorry,' George said lamely.

'What are you apologizing for?' said Jos furiously. 'You're not her cook or keeper. I can't understand why you don't throw her out.'

'It's my charm,' said Meredith.

George smiled.

'You just encourage her,' said Jos. 'She's going to be hell to be married to.'

George took a bus half-way, then walked the rest through Kensington Gardens. It would make her late and that would infuriate her father, but her head ached and the strain of going straight home was too much to bear. The rain had almost stopped, but the March wind blew what remained in sharp gusts around her neck and legs. There was practically no one in the park, only a few children fishing hopelessly, and a coloured couple mooching along with nowhere to go and all the weight of the world on their shoulders.

She reached the far gate and turned into the road. As usual, she'd gone too far to the right and ended up an extra fifteen minutes' walk from the street that would bring her into the place where James lived. She strode briskly along, hands in pockets, her pony tail flapping limp and wet behind her. She overtook and passed a girl in a tightly belted shiny yellow raincoat who teetered along in high-heeled, black boots, clinging to a parasol of an umbrella. George snorted and pulled the collar of her black leather coat closer round her neck.

'You're late,' said Ted. 'The one day you choose to come to lunch you're deliberately late. Why?'

'I slept in,' George said and sat down, still in her coat.

'You were probably out half the night, though I can't imagine who'd take you dressed like that. I hope you don't think you're going to eat your lunch dressed like that, because if so, you're very much mistaken.'

'I'll leave if you like,' George said, and got up.

'Don't upset your mother,' said Ted, sharply.

The lunch got under way with both of them stonily silent. Doris sighed often, and shot lugubrious, accusing glances at both of them.

'What a crowd they had there today,' she said, mournfully, after the soup was finished. 'I've asked Mrs L. that often to tell me when she's going to have a lot extra but she don't take a blind bit of notice. If there's not enough I catch it and if there's too much she complains about the bills. She don't know her own mind.'

'Leave,' said George.

'Now George,' her mother said, warningly. She waited nervously to see if George was going to continue, half hoping she would, then sighed when she didn't. 'I don't know, I'm sure,' she said, with an air of summing everything up.

'The trouble with you,' said Ted, cutting his meat viciously, 'is that you don't realize how lucky you are, and you never have done. Living rent free in this beautiful house, everything you could possibly want and nothing to worry about. You'd have known about it if I'd gone on being a two pound a week mechanic.'

'Mechanics are well paid these days,' said George, slyly.

'You be quiet. You're a fine one to talk – you've had everything money could buy from Mr James.'

'Is there anything he couldn't buy from you?' said George suddenly.

'No, and I'm proud to say it. There isn't anything I wouldn't give a fine gentleman like Mr James. Not that there's anything he wants. He's clever enough to have seen to that.'

'Would you give him me?' pressed George. 'If he asked you to, and gave you £100, would you have me chopped into small pieces and presented to him?'

Ted thumped the table and rose to his feet.

'By God, I won't have you mocking Mr James. I'll thrash you if you talk like that again.'

George tried to smile, but failed. Her father was standing over her shaking with a mixture of what she divined as anger and fear. He'd always been afraid. She wanted to ask him why he was frightened, to explain that James wasn't the Almighty and didn't need blood sacrifices. Maybe it was James's actual humanity that frightened him – maybe he saw, as she jibed or mocked, that James was only a big, fat fool and that his whole life had been dedicated to a mere man and not someone unique. His failure as a man must stare him in the face, his repeated cowardice rise up and stick out its tongue at him.

They finished lunch and Ted went out into the garden to weed. George helped her mother clear away and wash up. There wasn't even the antagonism that existed in her relationship with her father to warm that with her mother. She was embarrassed when alone with her, and had either to resort to banter or prompt her to come out with one of the endless grumbles against the Leamingtons that forever trembled on her lips, so that she would use George only as a listener and require no reply. She was sorry for her mother, but she didn't like her. She couldn't like anyone so utterly spineless and abject. Her mother hadn't even the excuse that her father had, because she hated James as much as Ted worshipped him. And she despised Ted. Her whole existence was a lesson in hypocrisy, hideously corroded with the bitter need for it over all those years.

'Meredith's getting married,' George said. Her mother had met Meredith once when she'd made the big mistake of bringing her home to lunch. Meredith had sat in bored silence and smoked throughout the meal. 'She's having a baby,' she added, without knowing why.

'Well,' was all Doris said. She seemed offended that George had told her. 'I hope you'll be careful I'm sure. Mr James would never forgive Ted if anything like that happened to you.' George dried the gravy tureen tenderly.

'Who's the fellow then?'

'He's called Jos. I don't know his surname.'

'Why doesn't he call himself Joseph properly?' said Doris, crossly.

'Why don't you call me Georgina?' said George.

Doris ran the hot water tap full blast. 'Your name's nothing to do with me and you know it. It was your father and Mr James.'

'You were my mother weren't you? Why didn't you say you didn't want to call me after that bloated slob.'

'George!' Doris stood quite still, listening fearfully to see if Ted or anyone else had been near the kitchen. She had one hand pressed protectively to her aproned heart.

'Oh, mother,' said George wearily, 'you're worse than dad. You act as though James was somebody.'

She wandered out into the garden where Ted was fiercely hoeing as though every weed that came up was a personal insult to James. She imagined herself saying, 'Dad, James has asked me to be his mistress and I've decided to accept. We're going to have a baby and call it Teddykins after you.'

She turned away and shouted to her mother that she was going. It occurred to her, as she passed through the house, that James must be waiting for an answer. He was quite likely to turn up again and ask for one. She stood uncertainly in the hall, then went upstairs to her dancing room. It was cold and bare, and the light reflected from the mirrors was an ugly, grey sheen. She sat at the piano and thought about writing him a note. Absently, she tinkled a tune, then let her fingers run haywire up and down the keyboard, just making a noise and nothing more.

She saw James in one of the mirrors before he spoke. He looked like an inquisitor.

'Your father said you'd just gone,' said James sternly.

'Did he now,' said George lightly, 'and what are you going to do about that – pull his fingernails out for telling a lie?'

'Have you decided?' asked James, heavily.

'Come here,' said George. He advanced ponderously across the room. She took him by the arm and faced the long mirror. 'We'd better practise just in case,' she said and started to goosestep to the wedding march, trying to drag James with her.

'Don't be silly,' he said and shook her off.

'Yes, I am silly amn't I? Silly-billy georgy-porgy.' She twirled with small mincing steps round him. 'Imagine I'm the sugar-plum fairy,' she said. 'When I'm finished you can pick me up and put me in your big, red mouth and roll me round your fat tongue.'

'Stop it!' roared James.

George stopped.

'Got a cigarette?' she said.

'You carry on like a bloody half-wit,' said James, giving her one. 'I'm not in the mood.'

'You should have a set of traffic lights on your forehead – green for go-ahead, red for don't trifle with me and amber – what could amber be for?'

James puffed his cigar, impatiently. 'You must have made up your mind by now,' he said.

George stared blankly at him. Somehow she found she hadn't even thought about it much. Seeing him there, asking her, it made it something which had to be seriously considered. There was nothing else in the room except the two of them and the emptiness between the mirrors and it was three o'clock in the afternoon.

She sat down again at the piano.

'It's so absurd, it embarrasses me,' she said.

'What's absurd about it?' said James. 'I love you and I want to live with you.'

George clicked her tongue in exasperation.

'Can't you see?' she said, 'look at us in that mirror. A fat, middle-aged man and a tall, ugly girl. We don't know anything about love. It's a stupid word to use.'

'So if I was young and handsome, and you were pretty, it would be different?'

'At least it wouldn't be laughable or indecent.' She paused. 'You haven't told me a single thing to show me why you should want to live with me. I've always been a joke to you. It's a sort of perversion wanting me. I just can't imagine it.'

James heard her say 'perversion' with a feeling of guilt. It wasn't that he wanted her to dress up as a nun and whip him, but there was an element of truth in the idea that his desire for George was slightly kinky. He'd hugged it to himself for years. There was something awful but fascinating in the thought that he could strip her naked and take her to bed. It amounted, he told himself, to a practically incestuous passion. But it wasn't just the sexual side. George was a freak. She was odd, peculiar. She was so awkward and looked so terrible but from her eyes he'd read a challenge, daring anyone to think that this was really her.

'Give it a try,' he said.

'Like a new toothpaste?' said George. 'Don't you want to get to know me first, kind sir?'

'I've known you all your life,' protested James.

'We've never been alone more than this ten minutes,' said George. 'You've never taken me out alone, or to the pictures, or even for a walk. You don't know if you could stand an hour of my company and I don't know if I could stand you.'

'Well, that's easy,' said James. 'Come on, we'll go out now. Where do you want to go?'

57

'If I went it would only be for one reason,' said George. 'I've got nothing to do. I'm bored. I haven't a boyfriend and I'm lonely. I'd rather go out with you than go back to my flat.'

'Understood,' said James. 'Let's go.'

'Where?'

'We'll drive somewhere first.'

She followed him downstairs. Her father opened the car door for them both.

'I'm taking George for a drive,' James said, 'she hadn't gone after all.'

'That's very good of you Mr James,' said Ted, looking at George hard to impress upon her that she must be on her best behaviour. He stood and waved as they drove off.

'Doesn't he make you sick?' said George. She could say anything to James now. There was no point in even beginning this unless she made the most of it. 'You can't really be so stupid that you believe you're as marvellous as he makes out.'

'I wouldn't pass too hasty a judgement on your father,' said James.

'Hasty! For God's sake, I've only watched him crawling and kowtowing for twenty-seven years. Don't you realize I've been brought up to think you a little tin god?'

James smiled. 'We'll go to Richmond,' he said.

They stayed out the whole of the rest of the day, doing very little. James didn't walk, he drove, so they drove through and round Richmond Park several times. He didn't look to right or left, though he several times commented on the beauty of the scenery to George, as though he was getting some tremendous enjoyment out of it. After his invigorating country afternoon, James needed refreshment, so they went to an hotel outside Richmond and had tea. George was told to tuck in. Then James drove very fast back to London and they sat and drank in the American bar of the Savoy. It ended with a long meal in the grill room and brandy and coffee afterwards. At eleven, James took her home to her flat.

When he stopped the car, George sat still, feeling stunned and vacant. She waited for him to kiss her with absolutely no emotion at all, and when he did she felt the usual excitement that she experienced when anyone kissed her, even in her dreams. She sat quite placidly while he kissed her again and his hands scrabbled around to find the openings in her leather coat. James was simple. He had no mind. He lived and slept and ate with utter conviction and he did nothing without economy of words and thought. There was nothing to get to know or appreciate.

'Did you enjoy that?' he said.

'I enjoy anyone kissing me,' George said. 'I'm sex-starved.'

'I meant the afternoon and evening. We were together almost eight hours. Does it prove we get on well? I probably wouldn't be with you that long any normal day so that's the most you'd ever get.'

'I'll let you know,' said George, and got out of the car. James nodded. He was confident. She waited until the car had gone before she went in.

Meredith was in bed, alone.

'You feeling all right?' said George.

'If that's meant to be sarcastic it's appreciated,' said Meredith. 'I'm in bed, alone, and I feel lousy. Where have you been? You never go out on Sunday evening.'

'Or any others,' said George.

'I kindly didn't say that.'

'Meredith, look at me. Am I really ugly?'

'Aw, for Christ's sake! I told you – I feel lousy. Do we have to go through that for the fifty-millionth time?'

The mute plea in George's big, long face made Meredith want to vomit and she'd vomited enough that day for other reasons. George was standing there in that terrible coat actually expecting her to indulge the usual self-pitying moans. She'd tried lying and telling her she was beautiful and unusual; she'd tried telling the truth. Now she simply ignored her.

'George, for the last time,' she said, 'have some pride. You don't go around in this life showing your feelings. It does no bloody good at all. You pretend even to yourself and then you feel better. Make me some coffee.'

For a moment she thought George was going to burst into

tears, as usual. She'd made, in many ways, a big mistake coming to live with George. Originally, she'd made the choice because she thought George looked as though she didn't give a damn about herself and that was all Meredith demanded from people. By the time she'd discovered George lived in one big emotional mess all the time, she couldn't do without her services as chief cook, bottle-washer and doormat.

George didn't cry this time. She made the coffee and brought it into the bedroom.

'Don't laugh,' she said. 'I've been out with a fella.'

'It had to happen,' said Meredith. She watched George closely. She wasn't exactly flushed with excitement.

'He wants me to live with him,' George blurted out. Meredith put her coffee cup down carefully.

'Actually, it isn't a man, it's a lobster,' said George. 'Big, red with shiny claws that he puts round you. He finds life difficult out of water and he wants me to feed him with shrimps and things. We mermaids are always getting requests like that.'

'I can't see your tail,' said Meredith.

'We're not exactly stupid,' said George, 'we keep our tails hidden.'

'Put the wireless on,' said Meredith. Humouring George was exhausting. She would grow more and more fey and progressively less funny. 'We're getting married on Friday,' she said, and went to sleep with Radio Luxembourg blaring and George doing a mermaid dance.

George said they should have Peg, and the members of her best dancing class for bridesmaids. Peg would wear pink satin with roses in her hair and the children would be dressed as nymphs and form a guard of honour with garlands of flowers. She herself would be a page in knickerbocker shorts and wear a cocked hat.

She seriously couldn't bear the thought of Meredith and Jos getting married in their lunch hour in some seedy town hall. They must both invite their parents at least, and have a nice meal somewhere, if they really wouldn't have a reception. It seemed to her very important that they should make an occasion of the marriage, if just to impress upon them what they were doing. Jos was half inclined to agree, but Meredith said in that case he could go and marry George and they could have their rotten pantomime.

By Thursday afternoon, George had to concede defeat. Anyway, Meredith was being sick almost constantly and was in no fit state for a real celebration. So George went out and bought all the most extravagant and delicious foods she could think of and prepared in secret a sumptuous meal. She did more than that. She went out again and bought Meredith a wedding dress. She got some very odd looks when she braved the carpeted acres of the hushed Bridal Departments and asked to see simple, short dresses to fit size 34 inch bust and 36 inch hips. They brought her lace and satin creations which would have drowned Meredith and which she would, in any case, have torn into shreds rather than wear. At seven p.m., with only half an hour to go, George strode into the teenage department of Fenwicks and lifted a straight, plain white silk shift from the rack. It had a small border of lace round the neck and armholes but otherwise it was strictly and severely unornamental.

She took it home shyly, and unwrapped the delicate thing from its whispering folds of tissue paper. Gently, she laid it on Meredith's bed, and rummaged around until she found the white satin shoes to go with it. They were slightly scuffed, like all Meredith's shoes. She put them on the floor beneath the dress and waited apprehensively for Meredith and Jos to come in.

When they did, George hovered excitedly around them until Meredith told her irritably to sit down and keep still and stop bumbling around like a fat old bee. Humbly, George sat and waited until Meredith would find a reason for going into the bedroom. In agony, she followed her to the door when she did and hardly dared to peep in to see what the reaction was.

Meredith looked at the dress. She could almost hear George's suspense. It was a very beautiful garment. She fingered it silently, and then, slipping off what she was wearing, pulled it over her head.

61

'You look lovely,' said George.

'Yes,' said Meredith. She stood looking at herself for a minute, then took it off and put her trousers and sweater back on again. It was impossible to say anything. If she enthused and thanked George it would all be too slushy for words. The deeper implications of the gift were something to shy away from.

'Thanks,' she said. 'It was unnecessary but very nice of you. I'll remember you in my will.'

It seemed to satisfy George. She sang as she made supper for them all and then chattered incessantly while they ate.

'Well Jos,' she said, gaily, 'tomorrow the secret will be out.'

'Which one?' said Jos.

'Mrs what – what Mrs will Meredith be?'

'For God's sake,' said Meredith, 'she's right. What's your awful surname?'

'That,' said Jos, 'is the most affected thing I've ever heard in my life. To pretend you don't know my name when you're going to marry me tomorrow is ludicrous.'

'I know,' said Meredith. 'I might not be able to go through with it. It isn't Grubb is it?'

'No, it is not.'

George clapped her hands. 'It's like Rumpelstiltskin,' she exclaimed. 'If you can't guess his name by midnight you can't marry him. You'll have to send spies out all over the Kingdom to try to find out. This is me being a spy.' She snatched the table-cloth and draped it round her and began slouching round the room hissing and shushing.

'Oh God,' said Meredith, 'tell us it, quick.'

'Jones,' said Jos, solemnly.

'You're joking,' said Meredith, aghast. 'No you're not. I remember now, you did tell me. Jos Jones. Mrs Meredith Jones. Jos, you'll have to change it. I can't give up Montgomery for Jones. You couldn't ask me to.'

It had the effect of making them all happy and close, George no less than the other two. The tension that Jos had felt disappeared, at least for an hour or so. It was a terrible mistake to marry Meredith and he knew this quite clearly. He didn't think of it lightly. Even before the baby was born they would be like strangers most of the time, and afterwards he couldn't imagine what disastrous results there would be. Already, he knew he must find a job, get out of George's flat, reach some level of security. What the hell Meredith was doing he didn't know. She said she wanted the baby and she wanted to marry him and no, she had no idea why. He kept trying to tell her what a momentous thing it would be to have a child, that she couldn't just do it because she felt like it. She said she could think of no better motive.

Jos forgot for a while and relaxed. George, for some reason he couldn't fathom, was taking a great delight in the approaching wedding, if it could be called that. He'd expected her to be moody and sullen and, he supposed, consumed with envy – not because he was any great catch but simply the fact of a marriage that wasn't hers and which emphasized her own single state even more heavily. He was sure no girl liked to see her friend get married, even if it was a marriage of haste and convenience. He watched carefully to see the cracks in George's bright and cheery façade, but there were none. She was genuinely thrilled and excited.

In the morning, they had to wait for Meredith to stop being sick before they could go to the Registry Office. She seemed to take an extra long time about it.

'We're going to be late,' Jos announced. 'Can't you hurry up?'

The only answer was a violent retch, followed by a curse. 'You can go by your bloody self,' yelled Meredith. 'Do you think I can help being sick?'

'Please,' said George. 'I'll help you get dressed if you feel better.'

'I don't feel better and even if I did I'm not a half-wit. I can tie my own shoe laces now.'

She came out of the bathroom, white and shaking, and lay on the bed. Nothing would move her. Jos settled in a chair and picked up the paper while George hovered miserably around offering coffee and toast and aspirins, but was refused with a snarl.

'I think I'll just go for a walk,' Jos said.

63

'A walk?' said George, incredulous.

'Yes. I'm not doing much good here am I? If she wants to get married she can meet me there at eleven. If not, see you later.'

Tearfully, George watched him walk out and turned anxiously to Meredith.

'You must go,' she pleaded.

Meredith went on staring at the ceiling.

'For the baby's sake,' she added.

Meredith closed her eyes. 'George, you're the bloody end,' she said. 'Just go away, anywhere.'

George trailed into the kitchen. There didn't seem much point in preparing her splendid lunch, but it was something to do. Unhappily, she washed the salad and made a dressing, then trimmed the three steaks and put them under the grill with a knob of butter on top of each one. All the time, she listened for any indication that Meredith was getting dressed, but she couldn't hear a sound. She put the asparagus in a pan. They said unhappy marriages were worse than being left on the shelf. She shouldn't push Meredith. But it would be so wonderful to be married to Jos.

'Meredith please!' she screamed, and then burst into noisy tears. She put her arms down on the formica top of the fridge and bawled.

'What's all the fuss?'

Meredith had suddenly appeared, cool and beautiful in her white dress.

'If you don't hurry up and stop making such a disgusting exhibition of yourself we'll certainly be late and it'll be your fault.' She picked some lettuce out of the bowl and crunched it noisily.

'You're going?' stammered George.

'Well, I'm not wearing this to be sick in.'

They hurried out of the house, with George wanting to run, and Meredith refusing. Frantically, George tried to hail a taxi but none passed them. All the way to the Office she was holding Meredith, disbelievingly, with one hand, and fingering the ring in her coat pocket with the other. Jos had given it to her as she was best man and bridesmaid rolled into one. It felt icy and smooth under her finger tip. She kept glancing at Meredith and noticing the admiration she was attracting from passers by and she felt proud. In her old black leather coat she must look a peculiar companion.

Jos was leaning nonchalantly against the stone wall outside. He smiled briefly at George and took Meredith by the hand. George stood back, tremulous, suddenly shy. They went up the steps and into a small ante-room, brown and dim with streaky grey lino on the floor.

'Got a cigarette?' said Meredith.

'You can't smoke now,' said George, shocked out of the almost holy trance that the sight of Meredith and Jos walking up the steps had sent her into.

'For Christ's sake,' said Meredith.

'Shut up,' said Jos. 'You can have it when it's over.'

Meredith tried to snatch her hand out of his but he held it tightly. She was still struggling when the clerk appeared at the door and told them he would like to check their particulars if they would kindly follow him. Relatives and friends, with a pained look at George, could stay where they were.

Jos stood up, Meredith remained sitting.

'I'm not moving until I get a bloody cigarette,' she hissed.

Jos bent over her. 'Look, you little whore, if you don't behave properly I'll give your backside such a belting that you'll never sit again.'

Meredith burst out laughing. The clerk stood waiting, crimson-faced and far from impassive.

They followed him and he started to check the licence.

'Your name, miss?' he asked Meredith, averting his eyes.

'Meredith Anna Montgomery,' chanted Meredith.

'And the names of your parents?'

'Penelope and Charles.'

'Alive?'

'I think so.'

The clerk smiled thinly.

'What you smirking at?' said Meredith. 'That's the absolute

truth. I haven't seen them for two years and they might very well be dead for all I know.'

The clerk went puce-coloured again, and turned despairingly to Jos, who gave the necessary details and added firmly that his parents were most certainly alive.

'How do you know?' said Meredith.

'Because I went to see them on Sunday and told them I was getting married and you were having a baby.'

'What a bloody lie,' said Meredith.

Hurriedly, the clerk led them out and into another room to the registrar, collecting George on the way. Meredith acquitted herself with honour, except for a half-smothered 'Oh God' when George started to cry in the background.

The registrar took his duty seriously for the registrar of a large London borough, where hundreds of couples were married, with little difference between them, and little interest in what the actual words of the ceremony were. His room was drab and colourless, but he had on his own account brightened it with what he considered the uplifting pictures of Rubens' 'Madonna and Child' and an oil done by a friend of his of a cottage in Devon. He always had fresh flowers on the desk and kept himself very smart. Once the room was filled with brightly dressed, be-buttonholed onlookers it seemed to him a festive and jolly place and every bit as nice as a church, though it wasn't his place to say that. But today was one of the sadder days when nothing kept the shadows and coldness at bay. The bride was pretty, but she looked cynical and ill, and the bridegroom had an air of rigid determination which showed he longed to walk out. There were no parents only a large beatnik sort of girl in a black coat who cried with despair rather than sentimentality. But they were 26 and 28, well above age, they must know their own minds. He hoped it wasn't a baby on the way, but knew it was. It wasn't his duty to tell them it still wasn't worth getting married if that was how they felt about it, so he tried to smile and be extra attentive.

They came out, relieved and hungry, to find it was sleeting. Again, no taxi appeared so they had to run all the way down the street and into the square and got soaked. Meredith took her dress off and got back into bed and Jos stripped his wringing clothes off and wandered around with a large bath towel tied toga fashion round him. George made her delicious lunch and they had it grouped round Meredith's bed, then Jos got in beside her and George went to wash the dishes.

Chapter Four

The only person George could talk to about Jos was Peg. She got into the habit in the weeks following the wedding of going down to Peg's room last thing at night, or in the early hours of the morning, or whenever it was that Jos and Meredith had retired into her room for the night. It meant waking Peg from her deep and concentrated slumbers but it was unavoidable. All she required of her was that she should heave herself up in her green bed and listen. George would squat on the edge of the bed and pour forth the day's analysis, slightly distracted by Peg's large, round steel rollers that looked as though they gave her head hell.

In the first month, Peg had been asked to believe that Jos was just about the most responsible person that ever walked God's earth. Although his shining soul was tied up with music, he had without hesitation got himself a job in a bank. When pressed, George admitted he hadn't actually given up any musical job to do this, but she explained most convincingly that what the job at the bank did to Jos harmed his musical talent, which was prodigious. He was also kind. He had absolutely insisted that George should accept some money each week, and he always *offered* to dry the dishes.

Jos's most outstanding virtues, however, were not really revealed until the third month of the ménage à trois, when George couldn't wait for nightfall to go panting down to Peg.

'Today,' she said, 'Jos came home with a – a cot. A cot, Peg!'

Peg regarded her, stonily. Sarcasm was a thing unknown to her and she had no idea how to deal with George's raptures effectively. She struggled for words.

'He's the father isn't he?' she said. 'Well of course he came home with a cot. Has it a hair mattress? That's what babies' cots should have.'

'Meredith hasn't even thought about a cot,' said George.

Peg stayed rebelliously silent.

'It's white and he bought some transfers to stick on the side. I'm going to help him. You have to soak them first. Jos is very artistic. Do you know, the other day he told me I had a face like the Iron Soldier. Have you seen that painting?'

'No,' said Peg. 'I wouldn't like to look like a soldier made of iron, anyway.'

'Don't worry, you don't,' said George, scornfully. 'Jos is very understanding. When I'm really fed up he doesn't bother me. He just gets on with his meal and I can sort of feel him being sympathetic. And he's got such a sense of humour.'

Peg snorted. 'Not very funny getting a girl into trouble. It's the baby I feel sorry for,' she said.

'It was Meredith got herself into trouble,' said George icily. 'I think Jos behaved superbly. He knew what she was like and in the circumstances he needn't have married her. He's making the best of complete hell. He never complains.'

'He hasn't got much to complain about that I can see,' said Peg, keeping her end up.

'You don't live with them,' said George, grandly. 'You don't see what I see.'

'I'd turn them out,' said Peg, stoutly.

'Turn out my best friend, six months pregnant, and her struggling husband? They've nowhere to go.'

'They'd find somewhere quick enough.'

'I think I'd better leave,' said George.

When she'd banged the door close, Peg snuggled down into the warmth of her bed. Their one-sided conversations always ended with George flouncing out, bitterly offended. Peg frowned and raised her eyebrows alternately in the darkness as she thought it all out. She sucked an end of one of the sheets in her mouth to help her, and when the wet, soggy taste no longer served to comfort her, spat it out. The way she saw it, when the baby was born, it would all work itself out.

This view was shared by Jos, when he was in an optimistic mood. For one thing, it would definitely mean moving. He had a feeling that if he said as much to Meredith she would only say what she'd said in the first place, that she didn't see why. George enjoyed having them. She would adore the baby. Her dancing class hours would give her plenty of time to take it for long walks in the park in the afternoon and she would be indispensable as a babysitter.

It was not that Jos disliked living with George. He hadn't really had much idea how Meredith managed to live with her, especially since he'd only had one disastrous attempt at sharing a flat himself. But he hadn't been there a week before he realized just how George manufactured the comforts of life for those who lived with her. Her organization was supremely efficient. She shopped, cooked and did the housework unobtrusively and apparently with enjoyment as well as without effort. It filled Jos with a sense of awe to find that his clothes were removed when they were dirty and reappeared a couple of days later immaculately ironed. He never had to wonder what he could fill his ravenously empty stomach with, partly because George saw that he never got really ravenous, but also because there were always things in the larder and fridge. Tins were never empty, bread was never stale. It was like living in a service flat without any of the bills.

At first, he was so overcome with gratitude that he felt guilty and was always heaping praise on George and thanking her. He didn't tell her she shouldn't bother, though. Then he started to take it for granted, like Meredith, and even to feel that he was doing George a favour by being there for her to look after. She would be so lonely without meals to cook and clothes to wash.

In the evenings and at the week-ends George carried out a policy of self-effacement. He and Meredith were, at first, out a lot. He hadn't much idea what George did, but gathered she spent most of the time reading and planning lessons for her classes. This seemed to him dull but in keeping and he supposed that she liked it. But as Meredith grew bigger she lost all her energy, and they took to staying in. George was nearly always there, very carefully not intruding. She sat quietly in a chair by the window and got on with whatever she was doing.

Out of sheer boredom, Jos was driven to talking to her. It started as a sort of teasing, but she took it so seriously that he had to stop. She seemed afraid to talk back to him, and would steal worried glances at Meredith, who couldn't have cared less. It took weeks for her to unbend and actually volunteer remarks and opinions, but once this happened they were well away. Meredith might as well not have been there. He looked forward to seeing George in the evening just to *talk* to her, about nothing in particular. She was his ally. He hated the radio and so did she and together they thwarted Meredith's desire to have it on all the time. It was the same with countless other things. In fact, Meredith found their combined company torture. She was used to George sitting for hours in moody silence, but when Jos did it too it drove her mad. No amount of taunting could break the cold front.

One hot August evening, when she'd tossed and turned heavily all day waiting for them to come in, they both ignored her to the extent of turning their backs and reading. Furthermore, they were both reading different copies of the same book and they were at the same page. Furious, she wrenched the books away and threw them both out of the window. With one accord, they each picked up part of the same newspaper, and when she had crumpled those into balls and hurled them after the books, they simply closed their eyes and lay back on the couch.

'Very clever,' said Meredith, cuttingly. 'Why don't you knit identical sweaters and buy a tandem?'

Jos smiled slightly.

'You're just so damned superior, aren't you?'

'I was laughing at your joke,' said Jos. 'You can be very amusing sometimes, can't she, George?'

'Sometimes,' said George, also smiling.

'Bugger you both,' said Meredith.

'I hope it isn't true that children are affected by pre-natal experiences,' said Jos.

'It isn't,' said George. 'The only thing that can affect them is anything that affects the blood stream because they're only connected to the mother through the blood supply'

'But doesn't anger affect the blood?' said Jos. 'I mean, suppose you keep losing your temper and the blood runs quicker – won't these repeated shocks affect an unborn child?'

'Shut up!' yelled Meredith.

'Aren't you interested in the miracle of childbirth?' said Jos. 'No,' said Meredith.

'Don't you want to understand what's happening?' said George. 'Jos and I could explain it to you.'

'I don't want to know,' said Meredith. 'You both make me sick.'

Jos turned to George. 'She probably won't even recognize labour when it starts,' he said.

'Oh, won't I,' said Meredith sourly.

'Are you frightened?' said Jos. George regarded her with interest. Meredith hated them both.

Another night, it was their stupid fooling about that made her want to scream. She kept trying to tell them that they weren't even vaguely funny, but they just wouldn't take any notice and she worked herself into a frenzy trying to make them stop it. They thought they were so bloody witty prancing around dressed up as policemen in a lot of silly clothes. They didn't even look like policemen.

'You look more like rag and bone men,' she roared.

'You 'ear that Fred?' said Jos.

'She finks we ain't policemen,' said George.

'We'll 'ave to show our cards,' said Jos. 'Here you are madam – just a peep, now.'

Meredith lunged forward and tore up whatever he was showing her.

'That's contempt,' said George.

'Obstructing an officer,' said Jos.

'Nine days,' said George.

They started doing a song and dance routine that involved kicking their legs up behind them and waving frantically at the audience. The big joke was to disappear into the kitchen, smiling and waving brightly, like the end of a chorus line, then collapse, jaded and bored, until the supposed tumultuous applause brought them on again as before.

'I can't stand it,' said Meredith, hysterically. 'O.K.,' said Jos.

They stopped and sat down quietly, exchanging looks across the room indicating that women who had nearly reached their time must be humoured.

'Put your feet up,' said George, kindly.

'I'm not a bloody invalid so stop being so patronizing. My God,' she went on deliberately, 'at least I know now what it feels like to look like the back of a bus and have to stay in every night.'

George flushed slowly and deeply, her eyes filling with tears at the reminder.

'You bitch,' said Jos, and crossed swiftly over to where George was sitting.

'Give her your shoulder to bawl on,' said Meredith, 'But watch she doesn't get too excited, won't you?'

'If you weren't pregnant, I'd smack your face,' said Jos. 'You'd think you were one of the world's beauties.'

'At least I'm not one of its freaks,' said Meredith.

'Maybe I'll smack it anyway,' said Jos, advancing towards her.

'Don't,' said George. Her nose had gone red with crying and her face looked puffed and swollen. 'It's true what she says so I don't know why I'm getting so upset.'

'Of course it's not true,' said Jos. He swore and kicked the leg of the chair Meredith was sitting in.

'It is,' said George, wanly. 'I'm ugly and big and stupid.'

'Oh God,' said Jos.

'I know,' said Meredith. 'It gets very boring doesn't it? She goes on like this all the time. The best thing to do is ignore her.'

Jos suddenly wanted to bring back his fist and smash it hard into her belly. He stared at her instead, imagining how her face would contort with pain, how the cold, self-assured little mask would slip. Then it occurred to him that she'd said those things to George for one reason only, and he smiled with malicious delight at the thought that she should experience such a very undetached emotion.

'You're jealous,' he said, softly, 'you're jealous of George. She's winning hands down, isn't she, instead of providing the humble audience you wanted. Nothing's working out right, is it?'

'I don't know what you're talking about,' said Meredith, sharply.

'You're jealous of George,' repeated Jos.

'How could I be?' drawled Meredith. 'Just look at her snivelling there. She hasn't got a single thing so how could I possibly be jealous of her?'

'And what have you got?' said Jos.

'Very clever,' said Meredith. 'So loaded with significance and inner meaning. I like the way you dropped your voice an octave.' She stood up, with an effort. 'I'm going to bed.'

'Good,' said Jos.

He felt quite light-hearted when she'd gone through into the bedroom. Sometimes, he wondered why he just didn't leave her. She seemed to want nothing from him except his presence. They hardly spoke, and now that the baby was almost due they didn't make love either. There was nothing but that great bulge to keep them together.

He tried to make allowances for her, just because George was always doing so. But none of the excuses worked. Basically, she was a selfish bitch with nothing to give anyone except her body. He didn't even miss that. He'd rather talk to George.

She was in the bedroom and he and George were free to enjoy the rest of the evening. He savoured the feeling, walking round the room and humming to himself. He wasn't bored. They wouldn't do anything exciting but they wouldn't need to go to the pictures or dash round seeing other people. He didn't know what they would do, or how to describe the active inactivity, but he would be looking forward to it the next night. He felt elated. George was still crouched in her chair, the picture of misery.

'Come and sit over here,' he said, and went himself to sit on the sofa. She joined him, reluctantly. Jos put his arm round her.

'We're quite an old married couple now,' he said.

'Us?'

'Yes. Don't you think it's seemed like being married to each of

the other two? I've felt like an eastern oil king with two wives –
one for sleeping with and the other for living with.'

'One for having babies,' said George.

'That's just to make her worth her keep.'

'It's a pity you can't have them both in one,' said George. 'I
mean, if I looked like Meredith there might have been a chance
for me.'

'Don't kid yourself,' said Jos. 'If you looked like Meredith I'd
kick you out of the window. I can't bear the sight of her.' He put
his arm lower and drew George to him. She turned her head
away and he turned it back so that he could look at her properly.
Her eyes looked down and then up, anywhere but at him until he
started moving from side to side and up and down, like a tic-tac
man, to catch their gaze. George laughed and at last steadied her
gaze to meet his. The doubt and unhappiness in her face made
Jos choke. He bent swiftly towards her and kissed her passionately.

'I – love – you,' he said separating each word harshly and
distinctly. 'I've never said that to anyone before. Do you believe
me?'

'Does it matter?' said George, trembling.

'Of course it matters. I've never said it. I've said everything
else but not that. Do you love me?'

'I always have,' said George, 'but it's useless. You're just sorry
for me, you're married – '

He put his hand over her mouth. He'd said he loved her without thinking what he was saying, but the minute he'd said it he
knew it was true. He was terrified she wouldn't believe him. It
was so simple to say, she might think he'd said it a thousand
times and it mattered very much that she should know he hadn't,
because he hadn't anything else new or fresh to give. She didn't
realize the value of the gift his tongue had just given her.

He shut his eyes until they hurt and tried to see all the weeks
that had gone by all at the same time, like a dying man is supposed to see his whole life laid out before him. Image after image
flashed in front of him. He could see himself going over to
George that first time and talking to her. He could see them

75

doing things together. They'd done it all as it should be done without realizing it – a long apprenticeship to the real thing. All that had been lacking was desire for her. He'd never thought he would feel that.

The aftermath that had seemed so important before didn't worry him in the slightest. He loved her. He could deal with the guilt and panic and all the endless worries that would tumble out. It wasn't taking advantage of her at all. He started to unfasten the shirt she was wearing, and pulled her skirt down. She was so excited that she clung to him and hindered him. He tried to unfasten her hold on him so that he could stand up and lead her to the divan, but she refused to let him, as though afraid that if she once let go it would all end. Urgently, he pulled her with him to the floor and lay on top of her, cradling her head in his hands. She was warm and soft and there was so much, so satisfying much, to hold and caress.

It should all have been so right. She was relaxed and wanting him, every nerve quivered with eagerness, but as he penetrated her, gasping with haste, he could feel her flinch and contract. He felt it but could do nothing about it, he was too preoccupied with his own climax. He wanted to reassure her, to stop, to go more slowly, but he couldn't contain himself and he had to go on leaving her suffering behind him.

She lay and wept. Exhausted, he wanted to turn over and go to sleep. He needed to gather strength to soothe and silence her.

'Sssh,' he said. 'It will be all right. It sometimes happens like that the first time.' He couldn't actually remember it ever happening before but then he couldn't recall having any girl for what was her first time.

'It didn't with Meredith,' sobbed George. 'I asked her once and she said it was an old wives' tale that it hurt. She said it was marvellous the first time.'

'Bugger Meredith,' said Jos, sleepily.

'I'm just no good. I'm as hopeless at sex as everything else.'

'Oh Christ,' said Jos. He couldn't believe the elation had gone so soon. He sat up and pressed the palms of his hands hard into his closed eyes.

'I'm sorry,' said George. 'I spoil everything.'

'Look,' said Jos. 'I love you.' He stopped. He couldn't think what he'd meant to say, or why he kept on thinking those words were so shattering. 'Don't let's talk now,' he pleaded.

He was scared. There wasn't anything to communicate by except speech. If only she could know how much he loved her, everything would be all right. But she couldn't. She had to be told and he didn't know how to tell. He wished he had a portable lie-detector which he could plug in and speak into and say 'Look, all those red flashes mean it's true.'

He flopped back on to the floor and groped for a cigarette. It was very undignified having his trousers round his ankles. He smiled experimentally but George didn't take it up. They made a sordid heap. Her clothes seemed to be everywhere. He swore when he couldn't find a cigarette in his pocket and said 'Oh Christ' and then 'Oh bloody hell'. He got up and stretched and yawned and looked down at her. He thought he would have to do something, temporarily. Vaguely, he bit his nails and stared down at her.

Then he heard Meredith cry out from the bedroom, a prolonged 'Oh', and then repeated again and again.

'She's started,' said George. They stared at each other, weak and numb, then the cry came again and George began to struggle frantically into her clothes.

'You go in,' said Jos. 'I'll ring for an ambulance.'

George pushed open the bedroom door and switched the light on.

'Put that bloody light off,' screamed Meredith. She was lying arching her back on the bed, her hands clutching her swollen belly. George felt a wave of sheer terror run through her, for herself, not Meredith, and then she moved forward and tried to help her off the bed and into her dressing gown.

The ambulance took twenty minutes to arrive. They sat, all three, on the side of the bed, Meredith in the middle, alternatively leaning on Jos and then on George, moaning and cursing them both. Dully, George thought it was like the ball game at school where someone stood in the middle and the other two threw the ball to each other over her head. She'd always hated being the piggy in the middle. She hugged Meredith and tried to comfort her, while Jos slumped on the other side. When the bell rang, he jumped as though he'd been asleep. On their way down, they passed Peg, standing at her door.

'I heard her scream,' said Peg, solemnly. 'Are you all right?' she said to Meredith.

'Don't be so bloody silly,' said Meredith. It was meant to be a roar, but came out as a feeble whisper.

'Do you want a boy or a girl?' said Peg, blinking.

Meredith laughed hysterically as they helped her into the ambulance, on and on until the tears streamed down her face. One of the ambulance men looked at Jos, 'Shall I slap her?' he said. Jos shook his head, and eventually Meredith's guffaws trailed off into spasmodic giggles. She seemed calmer, and gazed at them searchingly, from one to the other. Finally, she stopped at George, and her expression became mocking. She seemed about to sit up and say something, but another spasm of pain seized her, and instead she lay back, groaning.

George put her hand out to steady herself as the ambulance swayed round a corner. She found a nerve beating in the side of her head, and put that hand up to press and stop it, but it went on pulsating through her.

Gradually, inside her, a feeling of complete disaster surged up. It was a physical throbbing, welling up into her throat. She was sweating, and moisture rushed into her mouth from nowhere. She felt she was going to faint, when the ambulance stopped and the doors opened and the air hit her face. She and Jos clambered out stiffly, as though they'd been travelling all night on the back of an open lorry. They went into the hospital, following the stretcher men, and were left behind in the waiting room as they carried Meredith off down a long corridor. They sat down, hand in hand.

The nurses passing to and fro looked at them with just a flicker of sympathy. Maybe they think our only child's been knocked down by a bus, thought George. We're sitting here waiting to see if it's got to have its legs off or not. They don't know we're an adulterer and his mistress, waiting to see what the wife's had.

They waited four hours and then someone came and told them they might as well go home and get some sleep, it was going to take a long time. So they went back to the flat. The bed Meredith had got out of looked crumpled and forlorn, the covers twisted in painful contortions to one side of it and the pillows deeply dented. Jos fell on to it, fully clothed, and slept immediately. George went into the sitting room and sat up the rest of the night, smoking. It was she who phoned the hospital at 8 a.m. and was told Meredith had had a girl and both were well.

The relief of having Meredith out of the flat hit Jos the moment he woke up. She'd lain there, those last few months, like a great burden of guilt, a daily early reminder of his predicament. It was lovely to be able to stretch and fling his arms about and not hit her.

He could smell bacon frying, sweet and succulent, mixed with the strong hot wafts of coffee, and hear George moving quietly about in the kitchen. Quickly, he got up, deciding he would take a holiday from work, and padded through to see her.

'Good morning,' she said, formally.

'Morning,' he said. 'Isn't it marvellous not having Meredith moaning around?'

'That's an awful thing to say,' said George.

'Why? It's so obvious.'

'Don't you want to know about your child?' said George, stiffly.

'It won't be born yet,' said Jos, picking a piece of bacon out of the frying pan with a fork and holding it up to cook. 'I'll ring if you like.'

'I've rung,' said George, suddenly abandoning her cooking.

'Well?' said Jos. He felt vaguely excited, he was pleased to note.

'A girl,' said George. '7 lb 2 oz, at seven this morning, both well. You can visit this evening, 7.30 to 8.30.'

Jos sat down and ate his bacon. The only conscious thought he had was that it was a very good job it was a girl. If it had been a boy, it would have needed a father and George and he would have had to adopt it which might have caused all sorts of complications. But a girl could very well be managed by Meredith on her own with occasional visits from him.

He savoured the coffee and fatherhood. Somehow he automatically thought of a girl being like Meredith and that spoiled the enjoyment. He'd always thought of the baby as simply a child, his child, that he was responsible for and must protect. He hadn't realized it might make a difference whether it was a boy or a girl.

'What shall we do today?' he said.

'I have three classes,' George said. 'Aren't you going to work?'

'No. Neither are you. We'll have at least one day celebrating.'

'What?' said George. 'The birth of your baby?'

'Don't be mad.'

'That's the only thing I can think of that there is to celebrate,' said George, untying her apron. 'Unless it's your birthday or you've got a rise or something madly exciting like that.'

She reached behind the door for her leather coat and girded it tightly round her.

'Have a good time anyway,' she said, brightly. 'I'm off.'

'You're being – sensible,' said Jos.

'Yes,' said George, 'perhaps you wouldn't be in such a mess if you'd tried it.'

'Three cheers for you,' said Jos. 'You'd better go then.'

George hesitated. 'It's the only possible thing to do – I mean, for me to move out for a while. I'll stay with Peg until Meredith's out of hospital and you've found somewhere to go. Or I'll move if you like. It will be easier for me to find somewhere.'

'You do what you bloody well like,' said Jos, 'but don't think it will make me stay with Meredith.'

'But what about the baby? You cared so much about it,' said George.

'I don't any more.'

'What will Meredith do?' said George.

'Let her worry about that. And you needn't bother staying with Peg – I'll move out this morning.'

'Don't do that,' said George, quickly. 'It's perfectly easy for me to stay with Peg and you haven't really anywhere to go.'

'You make me cry,' said Jos. 'I'm not Meredith. I don't want to live in your lousy flat. Now go on, get out. Have a nice life.'

'I would never have thought you could sound like that,' said George, fighting against the inevitable tears.

'You started it,' said Jos.

'That sounds like a child,' said George. 'You make it all into a game of tit-for-tat. You don't seem to understand that I'm trying to do what's best for us. What good can it possibly do if we start living together?'

'Who wants to do good?' said Jos.

'All right, you just want to enjoy yourself,' said George, bitterly. 'Maybe you were better matched with Meredith than I thought.'

'Compliments will get you nowhere,' said Jos.

'Can't you be serious?' said George, desperately.

'Is that what you want?' said Jos. 'Shall I pace the floor saying my God what-are-we-going-to-do over and over again? Don't be so dreary.'

'I simply want you to think to the end,' said George, now openly crying.

Jos sighed and went to comfort her. She tried to shake him off, but he held her firmly and kissed her hair and ears and wondered why he'd so deliberately given her the impression that he lived for the moment. Anyone knowing the facts would think so too. Genuine mistakes arising from the best possible motives just didn't enter people's calculations. He saw he would have to plan aloud before George would relax.

'Speaking off the top of my head, old girl,' he said after a bit, as pompously as possible, 'I'd say the line of attack was as follows: wait till Meredith's better, sue her for divorce, see that the child is cared for, and get married. But we can't do anything until she is better so we may as well make the best of it and act as though she didn't exist.'

'You can't do that,' said George, dully.

'I don't see why not.'

'That's the point – you really don't.'

'Look – what good does it do blighting my life because of one mess? Would Meredith and I be happy? You know quite well how we live. Dedicating a mockery of a marriage to a child would harm it more than help it.'

'You should have thought of that before you married her,' said George.

'Christ, I know I should. I did, and I made the mistake of still thinking it might work. You can't keep coming back to that. It was only a ceremony anyway.'

The doorbell rang.

'Maybe it's the milkman,' said George, dabbing at her eyes. 'We owe him two weeks.'

'I'll go,' said Jos, thoroughly glad of the interruption. It was what they needed. He flung the door open with a flourish of welcome.

'Have you had word?' said Peg, lugubriously. 'I thought I'd ask before I went to work.' She peered anxiously past Jos for George.

'My dear Margaret,' said Jos. Peg frowned and raised her eyebrows in astonishment. 'Peg is short for Peggy which by some ridiculous linguistic quirk is short for Margaret, is it not?' said Jos. 'Anyway, come in. We have indeed had word and were just celebrating. Come and join us.'

He ushered Peg in and leapt for the half bottle of whisky he knew George had. Seeing Peg bear down on George, who was furtively splashing water on her face, he said quickly, 'George has been having a good old sentimental weep. She always saves her best tears for weddings, funerals and births.'

He poured three enormous glasses of whisky out and thrust one into Peg's hands.

'I don't drink,' said Peg, giggling so as not to give offence. 'I've got to go to work anyway.'

'Then I won't tell you about the *word*,' said Jos.

'I don't care,' said Peg, defiantly, but she had to know. 'How much of this do I have to have to know if it's a boy or a girl?' she asked.

'All of it,' said Jos. 'At one gulp.' He demonstrated and found when he'd righted himself that Peg had followed suit. He sprang forward as she heaved and spluttered and went staggering towards a chair. Her massive frame shuddered and the white of her eyes were turned up in appeal above her red, bulbous cheeks. Frightened, Jos patted her arm tentatively.

'It was hot,' said Peg, faintly.

'I bet it was,' said George admiringly, sipping her own drink. 'You shouldn't have told her to do that Jos. She'll be ill.'

'What was it anyhow?' murmured Peg.

'A girl,' said Jos.

'Oh. What you going to call it?'

'I don't know,' said Jos.

'Cherry's a nice name,' said Peg. 'I always wanted to be called Cherry. Or Candy. I was going to have a boy called Ralph and a girl called Cherry then twins called Valerie and Patricia.' She gave a vast yawn and Jos glimpsed her wisdom teeth far back in the wide pink cavern. 'I've come all over sleepy,' she said. She settled more comfortably into the protesting armchair, and her mouth fell gently open as she dozed off. The first snore sent George's whisky dancing in its glass.

The thought of having Peg lying there all day didn't appeal to Jos. He went down to lift her brogued feet on to a chair and dimly realized, as his head swam, that he too was suffering from the unwise gesture of drinking all that lovely whisky at one gulp. He smiled, and sinking to the floor leant his head gently against Peg's large, dimpled knees. His cheek moved softly against the rough silk of her stocking and he felt a sudden desire to miaow like a cat. In front of his smoked spectacles, he saw a fine and rare ankle, and stretched out his hand to hold it. His arm would only reach tantalizingly short of the thigh at the top. Struggling, he heaved himself on to his feet and peered at George. She was smiling.

'Oh George,' he said, 'you're drunk.'

George held out her arms and they embraced like two pregnant women who couldn't get any nearer because of their bellies. Jos closed his eyes hard, and opened them quickly which was a trick that gave him perfectly clear vision when he was drunk, for about two seconds. Greedily, but with great sense of urgency, he located the bottle and swiped it before the mist swirled up around him. He pressed it to George's lips feeling some trickle over his hand as her mouth rejected the overlarge dose he was putting into it.

'I'm wicked,' he said. He moved backwards to where he thought the bedroom was, but tripped over Peg's huge, hard toe. He heard George laughing and rolled over on the carpet, squirming, trying to see her. She was on the bed. He did his eye trick again and crawled like a lustful cat across the floor space between them.

They lay on the unmade bed side by side. George thought no one could say she was so drunk that she didn't know what she was doing. She did. She was going to make love and she wanted to. She remembered perfectly clearly about Meredith and the baby and how she'd felt about Jos half an hour ago, and she was consciously saying it didn't matter. She felt Jos undoing her leather coat and he was too slow. She tore off all her clothes and clasped him eagerly to her. Everything seemed on another plane, sight and hearing giving way to the intensity of her feeling. It was all just as she had imagined in the dreams where she felt she was having it – impatient, unbearably enjoyable, and then the sharp, exhilarating climax. She cried with the sheer joy of it, and as Jos pulled the covers over them she was longing for the second time.

Peg had never had a drink in her life. Her mother had signed the Rechabite pledge for her when she was six months old and she'd never looked back. It wasn't that she thought drink wicked, or even nasty, it was just that she knew she wouldn't like it. The same with yoghourt. She'd never had or even smelled the horrible stuff but she knew instinctively that it was not for her.

No one had tried to point out to her that there is drink and drink, and that some she might actually enjoy. Peg hadn't been to any teenage debauched parties, nor even to a wedding. Her lips were unsullied by even the drinks made specially for women who didn't really like drink either but didn't want to be thought teetotal. She didn't know, therefore, what effect it would have on her, so that when she opened her eyes and saw the bottle and her glass and remembered, her first feeling was one of amazement. That was what drink did to you. Many a night she hadn't been able to get to sleep and now she knew that if only she'd had a drink instead of Ovaltine there would have been no problem.

Peg had heard, of course, of hangovers. They were something, she had gathered, to be quite proud of, even though they were painful in themselves. She knew this because the girls at work sometimes said, to one another 'Had a good night?' and the answer would be 'You bet. Gotta terrible hangover.' George suffered from them occasionally and always seemed to Peg to be boasting when she groaned and clasped her head and announced that she had one. So Peg stood up carefully and tested each leg as though it had just come out of plaster before she stood on it. Next, she shook her head like a very wet dog, and rolled her eyes round and round. Gamely, she stepped out, swinging her arms and then came regretfully to the conclusion that she did not have a hangover. She just felt stiff and cramped from being all bunched up in that chair.

She looked around for a clock. She wasn't really worried because she'd never had a morning off in her life so the firm owed her one. There didn't seem to be a clock anywhere, neither in the sitting room nor in the kitchen. She pondered. There was no one there to ask if she might ring TIM and she didn't like to take the liberty. She felt she had to know the time before she went downstairs. She pivoted in the middle of the room and then thought George would be bound to have an alarm clock beside her bed. The door of the bedroom was slightly ajar. If she pushed it a little she could take a big enough peek to see the clock.

Peg peeked. George was naked from the waist up and her hair was all over the place. She had a blanket up to her waist. Jos had his pyjama jacket on that he'd been wearing when he opened the door, but his trousers were in a heap on the floor and if that wasn't sufficient she could see one bare leg sticking out. He had one arm curved round George's head, and the other was bent, the hand cupping George's left breast. They were both flushed and in a deep sleep.

She didn't withdraw her gaze in a hurry, partly because she'd always wanted to see George naked and had never quite managed it. If she tip-toed in she could do what Jos was doing. Undecided, she went on looking. She could say she'd only been looking for a clock if they woke up. But she would be embarrassed if Jos saw and thought anything, so she pulled her head back through the door and turned away.

Back in her own flat, Peg saw that it was only ten o'clock. She could get to work, by the tea break and say she'd slept in, which was true in a sort of way. Yet she didn't want to go to work, not with all that going on upstairs. She frowned heavily, and sat for a moment on her bed, with her hands on her knees. She'd seen which way the wind was blowing with all George's talk about Jos, but she hadn't thought it would end like that. George wasn't that sort of girl, though she'd always known Meredith was. George was like her, she was plain and didn't like men. It was all very queer. Peg got up and went out, pulling the door behind her. She stood in the hall, wondering what she could do. Something ought to be done. There was Meredith lying in hospital with the baby and those two lying upstairs like that. She thought of phoning George's mother, then she thought of phoning the hospital, but she couldn't think what to say. Other people might not feel the way she did, she'd just make a fool of herself and George would be furious and never speak to her again. Unhappily, Peg let herself out into the street and trudged solidly to the corner of the square. Here she paused, and looked back at the house, towards George's window. Naturally, there was nothing to see. It was just an ordinary window. Slowly, Peg faced the right direction again and plodded on.

In hospital Meredith came slowly round from her semi-drugged state. She made out the white blur of the cover and the black iron bars of the bedstead at the bottom. Her belly felt sore and bruised and the flesh around it hung in slack folds like a sail from which the wind has suddenly been taken away. For a long time she wondered if she had the strength to raise an arm or a leg, and when she eventually did the effort exhausted her. Without wanting to, she found herself crying, the tears running unheeded down her cheeks because she couldn't manage to wipe them away or turn her face into the pillow. Someone said 'You'll feel better soon, dear' and she stiffened. Warily, she half turned her head and saw a large, rosy-cheeked woman leaning confidentially towards her, from the next bed. It was a warning given just in time. She closed her eyes and concentrated on giving the impression that she was asleep.

A nurse woke her at teatime and she dreaded the friendly barrage her neighbours would set up. She really couldn't be bothered to think of some pointed rejoinder and it was so wearing to go on pretending she hadn't heard. The nurse was quite willing not to talk. She washed her, plumped up her pillows, delivered the tea, and took it away without comment when Meredith had spent half an hour just looking at it with loathing. A little later murmurs went up all round the ward and everyone craned eagerly forward, like a lot of dogs obediently slavering at the sound of the foodbell. Meredith turned listlessly and saw them bringing the babies in. The canvas cot at her side was filled with a red topped white bundle.

Oh God, she thought, this is where I have to feel maternal and loving. I'll have it adopted, immediately. She could hardly bring herself to look down at the thing which had given her such hell, and which she'd only seen as a messy, bloody ball held up at the end. With despair she leaned over and looked at it, then as quickly looked away. She was supposed to bathe and feed and clean it for years and years. She couldn't do it. They would have to take it away. She lay back fighting the nausea that seemed never to have gone, realizing that she'd made a dreadful mistake. It was impossible to work out why she'd done it. It hadn't paid off at all.

By the time the fathers' visiting hour had arrived, Meredith had passed what she was already terming her own crisis. Really, she'd behaved rather like George with all her tears and emotional upheaval. As she smoothed the coverlet with her hands and watched for Jos, she was thinking dispassionately this time about adoption. Jos might object, it didn't really matter. It was her child. She'd had it and he couldn't force her to keep it.

Jos didn't arrive until half-way through the allotted time. He had almost missed coming at all, because they hadn't woken up until five and in any case he'd felt no desire or even sense of duty about going to see Meredith. But George had insisted. She'd come as far as the hospital gate, making him buy flowers and chocolates on the way and telling him over and over again what Meredith had been through, what she must be feeling like and how kind and considerate he must be, at least for the time being.

But when he saw her she didn't look any different. He'd almost built up a vision of a dewy-eyed, tearful Meredith after George's graphic description. No such thing. She was very pale, certainly, and heavy eyed but her expression was one he knew well.

'Hi,' he said, and dumped the presents on the bed.

'Where the bloody hell have you been?' said Meredith – she hated to think how eagerly she'd been waiting for him.

'Sorry. I slept in. Had a late night last night,' said Jos, smiling weakly. 'How are you feeling?'

'Lousy.'

They sat in silence. Idly, Jos picked the petals off a rose, one by one. The baby let out a high, squeaky sound.

'Aren't you going to look at it?' said Meredith. 'This is your marvellous child that you couldn't bear being destroyed.'

Jos bent over and looked.

'It's hideous,' said Meredith. 'I hate it.'

'All new babies look like that,' said Jos. 'You wait till it's a bit older.'

'No,' said Meredith. 'I want to have it adopted.'

Jos suddenly had a terrible headache. 'Got any aspirins or dope or anything?' he asked.

'Not that I don't need myself,' said Meredith. 'How do you set about it? If I ask here they'll treat me like shit.'

'I don't know,' said Jos. 'Anyway, I doubt if I'd give my consent.'

'Then I'll leave it on a doorstep,' said Meredith.

'You're a bitch,' said Jos.

'And you're a bastard.'

'Why?' said Jos, sharply. Meredith had closed her eyes. He chewed his bottom lip viciously. They were on such bad terms it could do no more harm to tell her straight out that he was finished with her and wanted a divorce so that he could marry George. He didn't know why he didn't come out with it, perhaps a vague memory of George's instructions.

He left before time. The thing was, when you looked at Meredith from a distance, as he was standing looking at her from the door of the ward, she was so small and slight and wan-looking that you really felt sorry for her and wanted to rush over and comfort the poor little thing. It was when she opened her mouth, or when you got in close enough range to see the hardness in her eyes that you realized she didn't need comforting. She said her family and upbringing weren't important, that they had nothing to do with her, and he'd always agreed. But now he felt he'd like to know all about them to see if it helped to work things out.

'How was she?' said George.

'Fine,' said Jos, 'her usual glowing self.'

'Did you see the baby?'

'Yes.'

'Who was it like?'

'Just a baby.'

'Is Meredith proud of it?'

'Very. Absolutely bursting.'

'I told you,' said George. 'What does she want to call it?'

'Constance,' said Jos.

'Really? Why?'

'She thinks it's such a nice virtue.'

George laughed as they walked off.

'Did she like the flowers?' she asked.

'Adored them. Guessed immediately it was all your idea and sent her thanks.'

He didn't know why he was making up such a lot of silly rubbish. It would upset her so much to hear what Meredith had really said and a temporary deception couldn't do any harm, except to shock her all the more when Meredith came out and started talking about adoption. But, as he planned by then to have George safely removed from her influence, that didn't matter much. The important thing was to prove how happy they could be together, even without whisky, then he would have something concrete to base his arguments on. Furthermore, he was glad he hadn't mentioned George to Meredith. It would be far better if they simply fell apart as though there was no one else. He would wait.

Chapter Five

The day Mrs L. died was the same day that Meredith's baby was born, which, if they had been even remotely connected would have been very interesting, especially to those who believe in reincarnation. There was about her death the same abruptness and a similar measure of panic hung over the proceedings.

To begin with, she wasn't even ill. That is, she was the robust hypochondriac she'd always been, comfy in the knowledge that she had the gradual deterioration of all her ageing limbs taped. She had a touch of lumbago, regular mild bouts of heartburn, the odd liverish turn and a mixed assortment of recurring glandular disorders. Unlike most hypochondriacs, she had the unusual distinction of not relating what was wrong with her to her nearest and dearest, or even the absolutely distant. She kept them all to herself, gloating over them quietly, and presented to the world a glowing picture of health. It gave her great pleasure when people remarked on how well she was looking to know that it simply wasn't true. Even more peculiar was that she hadn't seen a doctor for five years, preferring the masochistic thrill of divining and prescribing for herself with the aid of a shelfful of medical dictionaries.

James knew she liked reading these tomes and sometimes added one to her collection. Actually, he was rather proud of her interest in medicine and used to tell his friends that there was no doubt Nelly would have been a doctor if she'd had the chance. That, and her beauty, were the two greatest comforts to him, and really he needed comforting because otherwise there was nothing but emptiness between them. Nelly was always pleasant. They had most of their meals together and she kept quiet or responded to his conversational gambits as he willed. She always looked smart and lovely, she did whatever he wanted with apparent enjoyment, and yet she had nothing to give. She was completely negative, and James could not see that it was he who had made her so.

She died with quite typical consideration. James had gone to a race meeting with Ted in tow, and they arrived back about 7 p.m., hungry but satisfied. James was satisfied because one of his horses had won two lucrative races, and Ted was satisfied because he'd been present. There was a cold but very appetizing supper laid out in the dining room, which James prevailed upon Ted to share, man to man. He had been particularly nice and considerate to Ted for some time lately. They polished off practically a whole cold chicken, an enormous salad, some liver pâté, cheese and a bottle of Nuit St Georges. Then Ted made coffee in the electric percolator on the sideboard, and they sat drinking port and smoking cigars. It was one of Ted's big moments and James relished the fact almost as much as he.

'I haven't seen George lately,' James said, when they'd finished the first glass of port.

'Nor have we,' said Ted. An edge of gloom threatened to creep over his enjoyment. 'You wouldn't think we were her parents the way she hardly ever comes in, even when she's here for her classes.' He sighed. 'I don't mind telling you, Mr James, she's a great disappointment to her mother and I.'

'Oh I don't know,' said James.

'She is, really. She's not something we can be proud of, going around the way she does. I've tried to talk to her, but she won't listen.' He paused. 'Funny how it's turned out,' he said, and then gaining courage from James's sympathetic puffing at his cigar, he added, 'You know, I used to dream of your son marrying my daughter – I could see it, plain as anything, even though I knew it could never have happened, we being what we are, even if you'd had a son.'

'I never had any children,' said James.

'I didn't mean to bring it up,' said Ted, confused. He knew how very much James minded his lack of children.

It was then that Doris came in and announced with no finesse at all that Mrs L. had been taken ill an hour ago and was now dead upstairs. Ted laid into her afterwards furiously for the way she'd gone about it, just blurting it out, like that. He said she should have told him first and he would have broken it as he thought it should be broken.

Doris, it appeared, had been putting out their supper when she'd heard a crash upstairs. She thought it was the cat pulling over the flower vase on the landing and had gone upstairs, swearing. Mrs L. was lying beside her bed with a medical dictionary flung on the floor beside her. The doctor had got there in fifteen minutes, which considering it was the rush hour was good going, but Doris had known she was quite dead before then. Her face was blue and pinched, and there was a thin trickle of blood coming out of her nose and ears. After the doctor had gone, she'd rushed out to find someone to help her lay Mrs L. out properly. Ted stopped her going into the details of such an unnecessary errand It was a slight on James to think she'd behaved like any common woman dashing into the street instead of demanding that the doctor should take care of everything.

While Doris was telling her tale and Ted was bickering with her, James was trying to pluck up the courage to go and see the dead Nelly. He was so overcome with horror at the thought that he felt no grief at all. It was expected of him to go and see her. He told Ted and Doris to stay where they were and walked stiffly up the stairs as though on parade. Outside Nelly's bedroom door, he stood still, his heart thudding uncomfortably high in his chest. He cleared his throat as the sweat started to gather on his forehead, and at last opened the door. He stepped in, closed it loudly, and stood with his eyes tight shut for five minutes before groping behind him for the door handle. He found it, opened the door again, stepped out and opened his aching eyes.

Downstairs, he said huskily, 'She looked very peaceful.'

Doris kept quiet. She didn't think Mrs L. looked in the least bit peaceful. In fact, she looked to Doris as though she'd had a few very bad moments indeed.

'Did she suffer much?'

'It was thrombosis – the heart,' said Doris, and was about to elaborate when Ted cut her short.

'A quick and merciful death,' he said, soothingly.

'Thank God,' said James.

'She probably never knew what hit her,' said Ted.

'Did something hit her?' said James.

'No, no. Only my way of putting it,' said Ted. 'I meant she didn't have time to realize what was happening before it was all over.'

'What do we do now?' said James.

'I'll take care of everything sir,' said Ted, instantly. 'You've had a dreadful shock. Why don't you go and lie down? Reaction might set in any moment – it really would be better if you lay down.'

Ted had never enjoyed three days more in his whole life than he enjoyed those three immediately after Mrs L.'s death. It was all he could do to stop himself singing as he went about the work of arranging the funeral and seeing to everything. He was indispensable to James, who didn't seem able to do or say anything except to tell Ted to look after things. Ted guarded what he called 'the privacy of mourning' zealously. He took James all his meals, sat with him in the evenings, wrote letters for him to sign and patted him often in a comforting way on the shoulder – a liberty he'd never taken before.

The funeral was tasteful and quiet, the only flaw being the absence of George in spite of telegrams, phone calls and letters informing her that her presence was vital. She answered none of them. Not only did she not turn up, she sent no message of condolence to James, not a single word, and not so much as a bunch of daisies from her joined the heaped floral tributes on the day. Ted gnashed his teeth with mortification, though James didn't seem to notice, and covered up his ungrateful and unfeeling daughter by sending a lavish wreath of lilies with the inscription 'In memory of a most kind aunty, her ever loving Georgy.' It went on the coffin with the ones from the immediate family, as they were rather weedy. James looked very imposing all in black. Never had Ted seen such a fine figure of a man, so absolutely appropriate in dress and bearing, at a funeral. He didn't make an exhibition of himself, like some of them did, but conducted himself soberly and in a most dignified way. Ted was very proud of him.

Not that Ted was slow to perceive that it wasn't so much James's sorrow that made him so quiet as the suddenness of it all. He was a man who had always had everything planned, organization was his be-all and end-all. If he'd arranged for Mrs L. to die he wouldn't really have minded, but to have it happen like that was an insult to all he stood for. Ted understood this. If he died before James, he prayed that he would have time to make the approaching event apparent.

Mrs L.'s death, like so many deaths, wasn't really as appreciated as it should have been until well after it was over. Doris was perhaps the first to realize how very welcome it was. Without Mrs L. to harry and annoy her life was smooth and untroubled. The chip she'd always carried on her shoulder about being a servant was considerably lifted. It was like having her own house, with James as a rather special guest. She began to believe what Ted had always told her about being so lucky – not that she for one moment thought it could last. The snag would be somewhere, of that she was sure.

Ted had never been annoyed by Mrs L., so he was slower to share Doris's pleasure. It was only when he noted the increasing hours James required his company that it occurred to him this was because Mrs L. wasn't available. He was the only one able and willing to give James his undivided attention. He looked ahead to the comfortable years of this uninterrupted bliss as he felt his grip become surer and firmer. James showed no desire for anyone else's company. No one came near the house. He sat and drank and brooded, and didn't seem to have any interest in any of his various concerns. Ted saw nothing peculiar about that, but Doris waited daily for it to end and a new régime begin.

Exactly what was going on in James's head neither of them, of course, knew. Once Nelly was buried, the terrible fear of seeing her, which had hung over him, disappeared, though he had oc-

casional uneasy moments when he wondered if she really was
dead as he hadn't seen the proof with his own eyes. He then went
through a brief period of tremendous depression. It was not that
he missed Nelly passionately, indeed the feeling was only inci-
dentally to do with her death at all. What depressed him was the
continued silence of George, whom he had by now expected to
have installed in a nice flat somewhere and be enjoying the
pleasure of visiting her. It had been at the back of his mind for
weeks, a constant nagging irritation, but it didn't really trouble
him until Nelly died. Then it goaded him every minute of the
day.

He had seen her only once since the day he'd taken her to
Richmond, and had been so sure she would come round to his
way of thinking that he hadn't contacted her again. Let her get
in touch with him, he'd given her enough rope to find the way. If
he pestered she would just get put off. What had made him so
extra sure had been her line of talk during the dinner he'd taken
her to, and also the small but important fact that she'd made
some attempt to dress up. She wasn't wearing her leather coat,
she was wearing a green astrakhan affair, and she had on quite
a nice dark green dress and earrings.

'You're looking very smart,' he'd said to her, right away.

'Thank you,' she said. 'I had to dress up for my only admirer
hadn't I?'

That had pleased him and he'd ventured further.

'You know, you could be a smasher,' he'd said.

'You mean with time and money spent on me,' she said in he
didn't know quite what tone.

'Yes. I don't know any reason why I shouldn't be frank with
you.'

'Oh, by all means be frank.'

'Well then, you need knocking into shape. I've always seen
that. You're no beauty and nothing could make you one. But
you're unusual. All you need is a good stylist. I'll see you
get it.'

'That will be nice,' she said.

'You need confidence,' he'd gone on. She'd laughed, and he

asked what she was laughing at, but she'd said nothing. 'I'd give it to you,' he'd finished.

'I'm sure you would,' she said.

'You think I'm ugly, don't you?' he'd asked, abruptly.

'No.'

'Old then?'

'Not old.'

'Well, what's holding you back?'

Again, she'd laughed as though he'd made some great joke, but at least she wasn't being silly. She was sitting there, quiet and polite and treating him seriously. Long after they'd finished the meal, they'd gone on sitting there and she'd shown no desire to go.

'Don't you want to try me first?' she asked, abruptly.

'Try you? I don't need to. I don't want you just for that.'

'Don't you?'

'Certainly not.'

He was angry and embarrassed, and calling the waiter paid the bill quickly. He took her home again and she'd seemed genuinely grateful when she thanked him for the evening. She didn't come out with any of her bitter or nasty remarks, and when he said 'Let me know soon' she smiled nicely and said she would, but he might not hear for a bit because she felt she had to stand by her flat mate who was having a baby.

That was five months ago. It was absurd to pretend that she was going to turn up any day, and yet he refused to believe she had turned down his offer good and flat. There was no one else, never had been and never would be, there was nothing in life for her except her dancing classes and that flat of hers. She could never turn down the only offer she'd had, it just wouldn't make sense. A girl like that wanted a man, a home and a family. They wanted them more than the pretty ones.

To go after George again seemed to James a foolhardy line of action. What he really needed was to know what had happened all these months, to know what was going on, and to find out this information he needed a go-between so that she wouldn't suspect. The obvious and only person to fill that role was Ted. After all, he was the girl's father.

'How's George?' he said, one evening about two weeks after the funeral. 'Haven't seen her about recently.'

Ted turned a dark, angry red.

'Neither have I,' he said. He was afraid James had noticed her absence at the funeral. He didn't miss a trick. 'She hasn't been near the place.'

'What about her classes?' said James.

'She hasn't had one of those for two months, but mind you it's the school holidays.'

'Seems odd,' said James.

'She is odd,' said Ted. 'I can't understand her.'

'Aren't you worried about not hearing from her? Isn't her mother worried?' pressed James. It would be better if Ted sought her for his own reasons if possible.

'She's done it before,' said Ted. 'Takes these spells of going off for months, never saying where she's been or anything. She's very moody.' He made it sound a sin.

'She might be ill,' said James.

'Not her,' said Ted, 'she's as strong as a horse. Eats like a navvy and never ails anything, I'll say that for her.'

James saw he was getting nowhere rapidly, so he came straight out with it. 'I think you should go and see if she's all right,' he said. 'Find out why she hasn't been. Don't mention I was worried or she might think I was interfering. I'd rather she didn't know I worried about her.'

'It's a waste of your time worrying about her,' said Ted, touched by this further evidence of James's kindness. 'You know how it breaks my heart that she doesn't seem to appreciate anything. It's not as though she doesn't know who's been responsible for everything she's had. She knows, but she just doesn't seem to be grateful. She's been spoiled. It's terrible to think of everything you've wasted on her, Mr James.'

'I don't think it's been wasted,' said James. 'I'd like you to go and see her.'

'Well of course if you want me to, I will. But she'd be best left to stew in her own juice.'

James had made his point. He wanted Ted to go immediately,

but felt any more pressure from him would seem peculiar, even to Ted, and he might go to see George in the wrong frame of mind. He didn't want Ted to do anything but pay a fatherly call, have a chat, and see which way the land lay. Nevertheless, he was consumed with impatience when day by day went by and Ted made no move. He kept giving him time off, saying pointedly that he was sure there were things Ted wanted to do. Finally, he decided to go away himself for a couple of days in the hope that Ted's enforced leisure and lack of company would make him remember to go and see his daughter.

If James had had any imagination at all he would have realized that there could be nothing more completely phoney than Ted going to see George. It was something which simply couldn't be done casually, or without arousing a great deal of resentment on both sides.

Ted had in fact no idea how even to get to George's flat. As far as he was concerned she lived in some squalid region well out of his beat and he resented having to go there. It took him half an hour even to find the street in the 'A to Z' – he didn't trust himself going beyond Park Lane without it – and very much longer than that to work out a bus and tube route.

He walked into the square grudging every footstep. He didn't know what he was going to say, except complain about her not coming to the funeral or anything. Yet that wasn't what he had been sent for. He was on some undefined mission for James, about which he had not to let on. It was up to him to stall for long enough to find out what she'd been doing these last few months and how she was. He supposed he'd see the latter with his own eyes clearly enough.

No one answered his first two rings. He stood on the doorstep, his hat tilted aggressively on one side, a frown already settled on his forehead. With impatience, he jabbed his finger on the bell again, good and hard, and kept it there. A window sash went up high in the building and he cunningly stood close into the door so that George wouldn't be able to see who it was. He had no doubt that if she did, she wouldn't let him in, father or no father.

That did the trick. Someone came down the stairs at a pretty fast lick, and was breathed heavily upon by Ted who catapulted into the hall the minute the door was opened.

'Why didn't you come to the funeral?' said Ted, then he saw it wasn't George.

'I wasn't invited,' said Jos.

Ted flushed. 'No need to give cheek. It was a mistake – I thought you were my daughter.'

'I've always been told I had a pretty face,' said Jos.

'There's no need to be impolite,' said Ted. 'I rang her bell. Has she moved then?'

It was on the tip of Jos's tongue to say yes, but he decided Ted would have to be met some time. George was keen on family ties, whatever she pretended.

'No,' he said, 'she still lives here.'

'Is she out?' said Ted.

'No. As a matter of fact she's in.'

'Who are you then? Can't she answer her own bell or doesn't she answer anything these days,' said Ted angrily. He'd been put off his stride good and proper now.

'I'm a visitor. A friend,' said Jos, and went on standing there in front of this small, square, red-faced man.

'I thought you said she was in?' said Ted.

'I did.'

'Then you might have the good manners to let her own father in,' said Ted.

Jos took his time going up the stairs, which was natural but silly because it only made Ted more furious. He felt it was unfair to George to simply walk on and say 'it was your father dear', but he couldn't keep this angry little man waiting in the hall. There really wasn't any way of easing him in gently. So he walked into the flat, a little ahead of Ted, with his hands in his pockets to give an impression of nonchalance and announced the farcical words, 'It's your father, George.'

'Why didn't you come to the funeral?' snapped Ted, stepping round Jos. 'It was disgusting behaviour after all that's been done by them for you. I don't suppose you've got any reason.'

George had just got up. It was three in the afternoon but

they'd just got up after a sudden and prolonged post-lunch love-making session. She was feeling weak and a bit giddy, so that her instant reaction at the sight of Ted was that she must sit down. She sat, with a heavy thud, on the edge of a chair and tried to concentrate on the figure of her father.

'Why ever have you come here?' she said at last.

'You weren't at the funeral,' said Ted, still standing.

'But that was a week ago,' said George. 'Is that really why you've come?'

'Considering you don't have the charity to answer letters and phone calls,' said Ted.

'Do you want some tea?' said George.

'No. You haven't answered.'

George pressed her hands to her forehead. 'I was busy,' she said.

'Enjoying yourself most likely,' said Ted.

'Most likely,' said George.

'While others suffered,' said Ted.

'I don't like funerals,' added George.

'I suppose other people love them,' said Ted.

'I didn't see what good it would do,' said George. 'I mean, she was dead.'

'It's a sign of respect,' said Ted, 'to those who are left. I suppose you never thought of that.'

'I'm sorry,' said George. 'Sit down. There's no need to stand there.'

'Thoughtless and selfish,' said Ted, furiously.

'I've said I'm sorry,' said George.

'It's not me that's the hurt party,' said Ted. 'It's someone else you should have had the gratitude to apologize to.'

'I will,' said George. 'I'll write to James.'

'It's easy getting out of it that way,' said Ted, rather lamely. She'd given in very easily. Now that she'd admitted her guilt there wasn't much he could do. 'What were you doing?' he said. 'Your mother's been worried.' He was aware that Jos was smiling and making signals at George. 'Here, what do you think you're doing?' he said, glad to have something to work up his anger again. 'I'll thank you to keep out of this, young man. It's not funny. I don't know who you think you are.'

'This is a friend,' said George.

'So he said,' said Ted, glaring at Jos. He couldn't really stand there shouting at her if he wanted to find out what was what. Feeling it was a sign of weakness all the same, he sat down stiffly, to George's relief.

'How have you been?' he said, swallowing hard at the indignity of stooping to such social niceties.

'Very well,' said George, embarrassed and amused. 'I'll make some tea, whatever you say.'

She went into the kitchen and put the kettle on. Ted was staring at Jos with distaste.

'It's been bad weather for August,' said Jos.

Ted frowned suspiciously. He hadn't come to be made fun of. This young man looked just the sort George would pick up with, though it surprised him that anyone would have her. He was untidy and unhealthy looking and didn't look as though he'd been in the army. Furthermore, he looked a bit of a wog – nothing serious maybe, but he was very black-haired and sallow-skinned for an Englishman. His trousers were too tight and made of that denim and his shirt was striped. George would make two of him in size.

'Do you have a job?' said Ted, abruptly.

'Yes,' said Jos.

'Where?'

'In a bank,' said Jos. It was the first time in his life he'd said it without feeling ashamed. Instead, he felt that had knocked Ted for six, which indeed it had. Ted naturally had a respect for banks. He'd been expecting Jos to say he was an artist or such like.

'Why aren't you there then?' he said, still trying to make capital out of it.

'I'm on holiday,' said Jos. Daringly, he added, 'I'm entitled to one, aren't I?'

'Who said you weren't?' said Ted, quickly. 'I was only asking.'

'Quite all right,' said Jos, smiling. He'd scored again, although to what end he didn't know.

George came in with the tea. She'd listened uncomfortably to their brief dialogue, not wanting Jos to make a fool of her father. He was so obviously unhappy sitting there trying to look frightening and important. She appreciated acutely the effort entailed for him to come here and whatever his real reasons she felt unreasonably touched. It was an unsolicited demonstration of affection.

They sat and drank tea, Ted sparingly in case he compromised himself. Jos silently contemplated the addition of a father-in-law to his list of relatives and dependants, and decided Ted didn't show any signs of horse-whipping him or producing a shot gun so there was no need to worry about the penny slowly dropping. To call on his daughter certainly showed a middle class fatherly interest but Ted's attitude wasn't one of concern. Once he'd made it clear how angry he was, Jos felt he'd lost interest in George and had become just a stranger sitting there, still with his coat on.

Finding the tea wasn't easing things much, Ted stood up again and renewed the attack.

'What have you been doing then?' he said.

'Nothing,' said George. 'I'm on my holidays.'

'This a holiday camp then?' said Ted, scathingly.

Jos laughed loudly.

'There's nothing unusual in me having a holiday at this time of the year,' protested George.

'Funny place to spend it,' said Ted.

'The food and entertainment are very good here,' said Jos solemnly.

'Where's your flat mate?' said Ted.

'In hospital,' said George.

'What's wrong with her?'

'She's had a baby. I told Mother about her.'

'Are you the father?' said Ted to Jos, with a sudden flash of insight. Jos nodded. 'Ah, that explains it,' said Ted. 'I thought George had found herself a boyfriend at last.'

'She has,' said Jos quickly.

'Not the way I meant,' said Ted. 'She been looking after you till the wife comes home?'

'That's right,' said George brightly. 'She's coming home soon. With the baby.'

'You'll have some time to spare then,' said Ted.

'Lots,' said George. 'I won't know what to do with myself, will I, Jos?'

'You can come over and see us,' said Ted. 'Your mother would like to see you. And Mr James.'

'It's lovely to be wanted,' said George.

'Shut up,' said Jos quietly, so that Ted couldn't quite hear.

'I'll be going,' said Ted, 'took me long enough to get here.'

'It was nice of you to drop in,' said George, 'you must do this more often.'

Ted frowned. 'You're being silly,' he said.

'Me?' said George.

'Talking like that, as though I wasn't your father,' said Ted, 'it's silly. I shouldn't need to trail over here. It should be you coming to see your elders and betters. Mind you come.'

He went out without closing the door, and thumped down the stairs heavily. It was exactly the sort of run down dump George would choose to live in, out of sheer badness. At home, she had all James's lovely things round her, everything beautiful, house, decoration, furniture, everything. Yet she had to give it up to come to this. Well, it was something they'd never catch him doing.

It was with relief that he returned home, not because his mission was accomplished in the sense of seeing George, but because he was back to richness and opulence. He went in at the front door, with his own key, and saw with pleasure the wide, spacious, white painted hall, the staircase winding gracefully up from it and the bowls of flowers on the landing and window sills. Even going down to the basement into the kitchen to see Doris he didn't leave behind the luxury, James had seen to that.

Doris was sitting by the open French window sewing one of James's shirts.

'Did you find her?' she said, breaking a piece of thread off between her teeth.

'Of course,' he said.

'What was the matter? Anything?'

'No. She's been having a holiday, making a mug of herself as usual.'

'What's she been doing?'

'Looking after that girl's husband – the one she shares the flat with that's had the baby.'

'A boy or a girl?' said Doris, eagerly.

'I don't know. I never asked,' said Ted, impatiently. 'That's not what I went wasting my time for, now is it?'

'I don't know, I'm sure,' said Doris. 'I don't know why you went. It's not as though she's a child. It's not as though she hasn't gone off before. I don't know why you had to go off after her.'

'Because James was worried,' said Ted.

'Why?' said Doris.

'I don't ask him whys and wherefores,' snapped Ted. 'What does it matter anyhow. I went. She's been looking after this young fellow.'

'He's not staying there, is he?' said Doris. 'Not while that Meredith's in hospital?'

'I don't know,' said Ted, sighing. She always wanted to know the most trivial details. It annoyed him to death.

'What was he like?'

'A scruff,' said Ted. 'But he works in a bank. They can't be very particular who they take on these days, that's all.'

'Do you think he was staying there?' she pressed.

'How should I know? It doesn't bleeding matter anyway. You can't see anyone taking advantage of our George or even wanting to, can you?' said Ted, brutally.

'You've always had it in for her,' said Doris. 'She has her points.'

'Well I can't see them,' said Ted. 'She looked a mess, same as she always does.'

'Looks aren't everything,' said Doris.

'She hasn't got much else,' said Ted. 'She's not grateful, is she? You can't say that for her.'

'You ought to leave her alone,' said Doris.

She had more time now to think about her daughter. There weren't any menus to make out and labour over, no dinners to arrange, none of that endless phoning for this and that and never the right thing delivered, no laundry to supervise, none of that. James was easy to please. He ate what she put before him and he didn't have anybody in. He told her the very day after the funeral that he didn't want to be bothered with any household worries and he wouldn't bother her. She was to carry on as usual and ask for money when she wanted it, and he wouldn't interfere. There was no question, he said, of not trusting her.

Deeply gratified, Doris was extra-meticulous about her duties, but even so she had these long afternoons when she could call the house and the time her own. So she sewed or knitted and listened to the wireless and thought about George when she wasn't worrying about when James would get married again. George ought to be married. She was twenty-seven and no one in sight, but then she didn't make the best of herself and Ted nagging on had never helped. She remembered once, when George was sixteen and invited to one of James's parties for the first time, James had sent her a beautiful pink dress. It had a silk bodice with forget-me-nots threaded round the collar, and masses of tulle in the skirt. George had been enraptured. She'd lifted it out and stroked it and held it up against herself, all starry eyed even though Doris could see at a glance that it wasn't going to suit her one bit. She'd said nothing though, and George had struggled into it and come to show her and Doris had said it was lovely. But it was no good. George had looked at herself and burst into tears, and taking it off, had hidden it in the box under the bed. Ted had been furious when she'd turned up for the party in her school skirt and a big blue pullover. He'd gone on and on, and George had pretended she was wearing them out of sheer cussedness and because she thought the dress was hideous. Then Ted had said something she'd never forgotten. 'I wish to God I had a daughter who looked like a daughter and not a navvy' he'd said to her, slowly and deliberately. Doris reckoned that was the beginning of George's real obstinacy. Nothing after that could get her into anything pretty. She seemed deliberately to wear all the things she looked worst in. When Doris bought her make up she threw it away. She wouldn't wear any stockings except black woollen ones, and any jewellery she was given was buried at the bottom of her dressing table.

Doris sighed. Looking back, she should have done or said something, given George confidence, but she didn't know how. Telling her she was a very pretty girl just made her laugh. She'd comforted herself with the thought that it was just a stage, that George would snap out of it once she started going out with boys. Only that had never happened. Stuck away in that boarding school she hadn't met any boys and she wasn't in any young circle at home.

That was the worst of sending her to one of them places, though Ted had been so pleased about it. She hadn't a chance to snap out of it. When she was at home in the holidays she spent her time writing silly letters to her friends and never seemed to have any that knew any boys. Doris remembered how high her hopes had been when George was sent off to a finishing school in Paris. She'd seen pictures of 'before and after' and knew what they could do for even the most hardened of horsy debutantes. George would come back wearing her clothes with a continental flair and wafting perfume wherever she went. Her letters had given a hint that this wasn't going to happen. They were full of references to art galleries and concerts and how awful the élite establishment she was at was. She came back one of the more outstanding failures the school had had, with her pony tail more bunchy and wild than ever, and wearing ankle socks and trousers. She was then nineteen and all hope was lost.

There was no reason why, in Doris's knowledgeable opinion, she should have turned out like that. It wasn't as though she herself was big and awkward, or Ted, or that she'd been brought up with a lot of brothers. She'd been a pretty enough little girl as anyone who cared to look at the photographs could see. It wasn't until she was twelve that she'd suddenly shot up and grown all lumpy. Even her face had seemed to change, to grow longer and fuller, all within a few months. But she still wasn't ugly, you couldn't say that about her, there were many far worse looking who found husbands. Doris wondered if she could suggest a marriage bureau before it was too late, though it didn't seem very nice somehow.

Doris heard James come in and put her sewing away quickly. She went upstairs and into the dining room where he was pouring out a whisky. She thought he wasn't looking well, a bit pinched around the jowls.

'You're back early, sir,' she said. She never called him Mr James like Ted did.

'I know,' said James. 'Is Ted in?'

'He's just gone to buy a paper,' said Doris, 'he won't be a minute.'

'What's he been doing with himself?' said James.

'The usual things, sir,' said Doris, surprised. 'He's been in the garden a lot and took the opportunity to give your clothes a good press.'

'Yes,' said James, 'but hasn't he got himself out? I told him to give himself a change.'

'Not really,' said Doris. 'I don't think he fancied going anywhere. He's a home bird as you know sir.'

James swallowed his impatience with the whisky.

'Have you anything I can eat?' he said.

'Of course sir,' said Doris. 'I'll have something ready in half an hour.'

'Tell Ted I'm here when he gets back,' said James. 'Make something for him too. He can eat here with me.'

Doris went to obey. She hadn't expected him till the next day, and though there was plenty to give him it was a different matter including Ted. At short notice you could make something tasty for one, but two cut out half the things she had in mind. Still, it was better than if it had been Mrs L. arriving home with him.

She was making a quiche lorraine when Ted came in.

'You're wanted in the dining room,' she said. 'James is back.'

'And I was out,' said Ted, pained.

'You're to go up at once and have supper with him,' said Doris. It was like telling him he was to dine with the Queen. His face lit up and he couldn't get there quick enough.

'Good evening, Mr James,' said Ted genially. 'Did you have a pleasant trip?' – as though he'd been away weeks.

'Yes,' said James, 'but I'm glad to be back.'

'Home's home,' said Ted, smugly. He took it as a personal compliment. 'I felt just the same this afternoon and I was only out a few hours.'

'Where were you?' said James hopefully, but Ted had launched into a long description of how he hated leaving home and why and what he felt when he came back. By the time he'd finished, Doris was bringing in some soup and he knew she'd be in and out until she'd brought the main dish so he didn't have a chance to ask again.

When the quiche and salad had been put on the table he repeated his question, feeling exhausted at the thought that he might be side-tracked again.

'Where were you this afternoon,' he said. 'Anywhere interesting?'

'I went to see George,' said Ted. James waited. 'Couldn't get much satisfaction out of her except that she was sorry about you-know-what.'

'What?' said James, tensely.

'The funeral, not turning up.'

'Oh.'

'I told you it would just be pure selfishness,' went on Ted. 'Said she didn't like them. I told her, I said no one liked them – '

'What's she been doing with herself?' said James abruptly. He didn't care about the funeral.

'Being a mug, as usual,' said Ted.

'How?'

'Looking after this fellow.' James raised his eyebrows.

'Oh nothing like that,' said Ted. 'You can't see anyone having our George can you? No, this chap is her flatmate's husband. She just had a baby and George has been looking after her old man.'

'What was his name?' said James.

Ted was taken aback. He expected Doris to ask such stupid questions but not James. He didn't quite know what to say. It seemed a suddenly obvious failure on his part not to have asked.

'I didn't ask,' he said, shame-faced.

'It doesn't matter,' said James.

'He was a scruffy sort,' said Ted, 'but he worked in a bank, so he said.'

'Was he staying there alone with George?' said James, uneasily.

Ted stared. It might be Doris sitting there.

'I don't know,' he said. 'But there wouldn't be any hanky-panky, not with George. It's her mate's husband, he's a friend of hers.'

'You can never tell,' said James, lowering his eyes furtively. 'How did they seem together?'

'Seem?' said Ted, puzzled.

'How did they act? Were they just friendly or could you see it had gone further? What did he call her? Has she two beds?'

He heard himself asking these ridiculous questions feverishly and he could see Ted sitting there round-eyed with amazement, not knowing how to reply. Shakily, James picked up his fork and attempted to eat the neglected quiche, not commenting on Ted's silence. He felt sure this young man was the one he'd seen with George that time. It didn't matter if it was her friend's husband, she'd liked him. He'd look if he was pipped at the post. But he was being silly. Ted's expression and what he knew about George told him that. She wasn't that sort of girl, but even as he thought that he remembered her over-passionate kisses and what she'd said, even jokingly, about being ripe for plucking. He'd been slow. He hadn't offered her enough because it hadn't occurred to him and anyway he couldn't offer it. He had an ace card to play.

'Ted,' he said. 'I'm getting married again.'

Chapter Six

Meredith stayed longer than the normal ten days in hospital. She'd had so many stitches that it took her some time to get over the excessive soreness after they were removed and that kept her in an extra four days. It also turned out that the baby had been born with a twisted foot because of its cramped position in the womb, but they hadn't told her, said the sister, for fear of upsetting her unnecessarily when she was in a weak state. It was really nothing to be anxious about. One out of twenty babies, large babies born of small mothers, suffered from this and with careful exercise were perfectly normal by the time they walked.

The last person to be anxious was Meredith, although it took those who looked after her some time to appreciate it, and even then they fought shy of being too hard on her. She'd had a very bad time, even if a lot of it was her own fault, and her husband didn't seem very keen on visiting her so all wasn't well there. They waited for her to gain strength and start to take an interest in her lovely daughter, as they'd seen happen so many times. But Meredith didn't develop according to pattern. She hardly gave the baby a cursory glance, and refused point blank to breast-feed it. Shown how to exercise its tiny, fragile, malformed foot she curled her lip and said it looked perfectly all right to her and anyway she didn't feel like holding it.

One by one, the big guns had a go at her. The Sister in charge of her ward, who'd a reputation for reducing patients to tears with a few irascible comments, but was capable of great compassion, tried at first to be kindly and patient, until Meredith read a book while she was being shown how to change the baby's nappy. Then she let fly, and asked her just why she thought she was the only one who was entitled to do sweet nothing for her child. Meredith said she wanted it adopted. Shocked, the Sister said that was utterly cowardly and a desertion of her duty. Meredith said she could say what she utterly well liked.

The Matron was more abrupt. She said, quite calmly, that it was not the job of the hospital to look after any baby entirely when the mother was fit and capable. She therefore told Meredith, after she'd been there ten days, that her baby would be put beside her and if she refused to feed it, no one would. The whole ward went through agony for twenty-four hours, except Meredith. She lay sleeping, ignoring the frenzied howls of the baby and the loudly-voiced contempt of her neighbours and the nurses. It didn't seem to disturb her at all. Eventually, a poker-faced sister snatched the hysterical baby up and marched off with it. Meredith examined her dripping nipples with disgust, and settled down to being sent to Coventry, which both amused and suited her very well.

The most disastrous effort to bring this recalcitrant mother to a full realization of her role in life from now on was made by the hospital clergyman. He was a Church of England vicar who enjoyed visiting and administering in the maternity ward very much indeed. It was all so nicely straightforward. The mothers, churchgoers or not, were usually eager to join in short prayers for their babies out of sheer happiness or relief that it was all over. Occasionally, there was a sad case of a baby dying, and then he had a heartbreaking time showing the mother, very gently, how God moved in a mysterious way. But on the whole it was a happy place.

The minister noted that Meredith had two 'A's on her record card – A for Atheist and A for 'Awkward'. The latter could mean anything from being five minutes late for her ante-natal appointments to refusing to take her iron pills, so he wasn't too alarmed by it. When the position was explained to him by an icy-voiced sister, he looked also for a 'U', meaning unmarried mother, but there wasn't one. He was used to a difficult time with 'U's. Kindly, he approached Meredith's bed, smiling and shifting his glasses more securely up his nose to get a better look at her. She looked very small and pale to have two A's. Meredith looked up and as quickly down again at the lurid paper-back she was reading.

'I'm an atheist,' she said. 'You've got the wrong bed.'

'Well, I've come to see you as a friend, not necessarily as a minister of religion,' said the vicar gently.

'Look,' said Meredith, decisively. 'I loathe chit-chat. I don't specially want to be rude, but I've absolutely no desire to talk to you at all, so I'm afraid that you'll have to respect that even if you want to talk to me. If you go on, I'll simply put my ear phones on until you've gone and have a basinful of Mrs Dale.'

The vicar tried to hold her gaze and said very sorrowfully, 'My dear, what are you afraid of?'

'Christ!' said Meredith, and carried out her threat.

The sight of the vicar shaking his head from side to side and voicing words of admonition and comfort that she couldn't hear made her laugh for the first time since she'd come into hospital. At that, the vicar got up and left, looking like a long-eared, reproachful spaniel.

They made a concerted attempt, of course, through Jos, but this was a most unrewarding experience. The sister caught him as he was about to go in one evening – quarter of an hour before the end, and only then because George insisted.

'I'd like a word with you Mr Jones,' she said, firmly.

'Certainly,' said Jos with alacrity, eager to escape even those few minutes with Meredith.

He followed her into her office.

'Your wife refuses to have anything to do with her baby,' said the sister abruptly. 'Do you know why?'

'She's a bitch,' said Jos.

The sister winced. 'I'm sorry,' said Jos, 'but that's absolutely the long and short of it. God knows why she took it into her head to have it, but she did and now she's just reverting to type.'

'Did you know she wants it adopted?' said the sister.

'Yes.'

'What do you think about that?'

'It's a shame,' said Jos. The sister brightened. 'But it's probably the only solution.'

'Haven't you any feelings as a father?' pleaded the sister.

'Well, I did have,' said Jos, 'but not now. It would be difficult anyway. I mean, I haven't told Meredith yet, but I'm living with someone else and I want to marry her so I'll have to get a divorce. I don't think having a baby around would make my marriage very happy.'

The sister gave up in despair and disgust, and the bitter reflection that if babies went to those who deserved them, the world would be a lot better off.

Jos knew, of course, that keeping his daughter might not make his proposed marriage to George happy, but it would be what she would insist on if she found out that she was to be given away for adoption. As it was, her devotion to a baby she'd never seen went almost beyond the bounds of decency. She knitted all the time for her, spent hours suggesting names, and kept pressing Jos to get more of the equipment she would need when she came out of hospital. Jos therefore found himself Meredith's ally. He too wanted the baby removed to Dr Barnardo's or somewhere as quickly as possible and with any hope of tracing it doomed to failure. His conscience gave him hell, which he miserably knew it ought to do. Confronted with the papers Meredith had somehow obtained, he thought wildly of taking the baby home to his mother, or Meredith's mother, anyone's mother. It didn't seem such a bad idea to keep it and give it into George's tender care. But at such signs of weakness, Meredith frothed at the mouth and screamed at him until she'd made him write his signature in the appropriate place.

That over, there was left the problem of how to break it to Meredith that he wanted a divorce and by comparison signing away his child seemed nothing. She was cussed and vicious enough to refuse just for the hell of it, not because she really cared about him, and then there would be no getting round her. A meeting between George and her was what he most dreaded. She would pounce on all the conscience-stricken doubts that lay so nakedly on the surface and twist and direct them as she willed, until George would run away from him, forgetting how right it all seemed when they were together. Yet Meredith would go to the flat the minute she left hospital and George would still be there unless he did something very quickly.

The day before Meredith was due to come out, he tried to do it.

'I think we ought to leave London,' he said to George in the middle of their supper. 'Tomorrow – just pack our bags and go. Emigrate.'

George went on eating.

'What do you think?' he demanded.

'I think,' said George slowly, 'that must mean Meredith and the baby are coming home tomorrow.'

'That's purely incidental,' said Jos.

'Well, it can stay incidental. It isn't going to help running away from them. What would poor Meredith do, left in the lurch with a poor baby like that? Don't be a cad sir,' said George.

'If there was no baby, would you still feel the same?' asked Jos, nervously.

'As there is, there's no point in thinking about it.'

Jos sensed that was as good as admitting that it was Meredith's plight as a mother which was weighing most heavily with George. He closed his eyes tightly, and tried to estimate, soberly and realistically, the pros and cons of telling her that the baby had been adopted. It was impossible to judge what reactions would follow her first emotional impulse, which was bound to be violent.

'We must wait until Meredith and the baby are stronger,' said George placidly, 'then we must all have a serious conference and put our cards on the table.'

'Sounds like a campaign to launch trading stamps,' said Jos bitterly. 'I'm really looking forward to it. Where are you getting the round table and the Happy Families pack?'

'We must be fair,' said George.

'Oh, definitely,' said Jos, 'that's most important. I wouldn't like not to be fair. It would be jolly bad form.'

'There's no need to go on like that,' said George.

'What's going to be the outcome of your little shareholders' meeting?' said Jos. 'I suppose you expect Meredith to lift her chin bravely, and say you're absolutely right old thing, you and Jos must get together, it was all a dashed awkward mistake. All I want is 2½d. a week to keep myself and the baby and what about its daddy visiting it Tuesdays and Thursdays. Best of luck, mates, and no hard feeling.' He stopped for breath. 'Is that what you expect?'

'Not exactly,' said George, flushing slightly.

'Good,' said Jos, 'because then you won't be disappointed. I'll tell you something else – you won't get as far as laying cards on tables because before that Meredith will have bust us up good and proper. You seem to imagine we can all live together, tra la, in a cosy little threesome while things miraculously sort themselves out. For God's sake, George, don't be so bloody stupid. The three of us couldn't last together without tearing each other's eyes out for more than five minutes.'

'We did before the baby came,' said George, defensively.

'Like hell,' said Jos, furiously, 'and in any case you were the odd one out, on the surface. Do you think Meredith will sleep on this divan while you sleep with me? Do you?'

'No,' said George. 'I thought you could sleep there at first.'

'You did,' said Jos flatly. 'How many more cosy little arrangements have you been making secretly? Do I eat in the kitchen and wash in the sink?'

'Oh Jos, don't be so awkward,' said George, 'I'm only trying to make the best of it. What would you do, anyway? You wouldn't really walk out the day she came out of hospital with a two weeks old baby. Think of all she's been through.'

'We've been over all this,' said Jos wearily. 'I've told you – Meredith got herself into this and there is no point in wasting any pity on her. Our marriage was a ridiculous mistake and the sooner ended the better. Even you admit we couldn't make a go of it. Lastly, I love you and only you and I want to live with and marry you, but if you won't do it because of scruples over Meredith that still wouldn't make me stay with her. You're no homewrecker. I would leave Meredith anyway.'

'But the baby,' said George.

Jos took a deep breath. 'George, there is no baby. Got that?' he said.

'What do you mean?'

'Meredith had her baby adopted two days ago. You couldn't trace it now if you wanted to.' He waited for the storm, but it didn't come.

'Why?' said George.

'She hated it. She wouldn't feed or look at it from the very first day. She refused to have anything to do with it. She said it had all been a tactical error and that was that.'

'I don't believe it,' said George. 'A tiny baby – '

'Of course you believe it,' said Jos, cruelly. 'You know quite well that it's just how one would expect a bitch like Meredith to behave. And before you start on me, I'd better tell you that I signed those adoption papers not just because Meredith insisted but because I thought it was the best thing to do. It will go to a good home to people who will love it. Our life would get an impossible start with someone else's child round our necks.'

'She isn't someone else's,' said George, 'she's yours.'

'And Meredith's.'

'That doesn't make any difference. If Meredith rejects her, it's up to you to love her all the more. If you don't get her back, Jos, I'll never speak to you again. I mean that. I couldn't live for a moment with anyone who gave their child away because it must mean he lacked any love or real feeling and was utterly selfish.'

'It doesn't mean that at all,' said Jos. 'I love you and that's why I did it.'

'How can you blame me?' said George, excitedly. 'I would love to look after your baby and you know it.'

'Exactly,' said Jos, 'it would always divide us. It would be *my* baby, not our baby.'

'Stop calling her "it",' said George. 'I don't want to argue. If you don't get your daughter back immediately, I'm leaving you.'

'I can't,' said Jos. 'I signed the papers.'

'Adoptions aren't done so quickly,' said George, sharply.

'There's a six week period during which you can change your mind. I'm sure of it.'

'You're just being sentimental,' said Jos. 'I'm not a monster, George. I felt terrible signing it – her – away. I did really. I couldn't sleep the night before for thinking about it.'

'Oh, poor little boy, did he have to give away his toy car?' said George, shaking with anger and contempt. 'You bastard.'

'George, please – we couldn't have a happy marriage with that baby as a responsibility.'

'Of course we could. Other marriages have begun with babies from a first marriage and been perfectly happy. I would love her like my own. She's only two weeks old, Jos, she's not a fully grown Meredith coming to live with us. She'll grow up to be a person in her own right. We'll have other children and we won't even remember she's any different.'

'She's got a deformed foot,' said Jos, horrified at himself. He knew he was only saying it to make himself sound an even bigger bastard and to see how George would enjoy the revelation, how it would add such poignant depth to her pleading. He couldn't resist piling it on.

'Oh how awful,' said George, 'how terrible. Oh Jos, the poor little thing, imagine not being wanted *and* having a deformed foot.'

'And it's coloured. With one eye,' said Jos, and burst out laughing at George's fleeting expression of belief, horror, compassion. He stopped, with an effort. 'I'm sorry,' he said. 'Its foot's not actually deformed, I'm afraid. It just got twisted inside Meredith. You can't see anything, it just looks like an ordinary foot. The nurse said it just needed regular exercising and by the time it walked you wouldn't notice the difference, it would be perfectly all right. Sorry to disappoint you.'

'What are you playing at?' said George. She was sitting very stiff and erect, completely white-faced and still.

'Nothing,' said Jos. He fiddled unhappily with the tablecloth.

'How can you make fun of your baby's deformity?'

'Oh shut up,' said Jos, getting up. 'How can I this, how can I that. You're so self-righteous it's killing me. You sit there giving out your sanctimonious judgements as though everyone else was in the wrong and cared about nothing. It's bloody sickening, I can tell you, and I've just about had enough of it.'

He shouted the last sentence without realizing that he'd raised his voice so loud. George turned away. She didn't want to reply or argue, but even stating her opinion in the most crystal-clear fashion ended in a row. She felt Jos knew she was immovable, that nothing could alter her determination both to have nothing to do with him if he really let his baby be adopted, and to meet Meredith, and face up to her, when she came out of hospital. But Jos wasn't so emphatically sure about anything. She could feel his weakness even before he started shouting.

'All right,' said Jos, 'let's be reasonable.'

'Willingly,' said George.

'Suppose,' said Jos, 'Meredith refuses to divorce me. What will you do?'

'Let's wait until it happens,' said George.

'No. You promised to be reasonable. It's more than reasonable to assume that she will, and once you're under her influence again you're hardly capable of knowing your own mind. I want to know now, when everything's cool and unemotional.'

'If she really wanted the baby adopted, and you agreed we should take her, I'd go with you,' said George.

'And if I wouldn't keep?' said Jos.

'I wouldn't go with you. I told you.'

'Who do you love?' said Jos, 'me, or this baby you've never seen?'

'Both,' said George, 'they're both the same thing.'

'Suppose,' said Jos, 'and again this is absolutely reasonable, suppose this baby wasn't mine? You know as well as I do that Meredith slept around. How does anyone know I'm definitely the father? I'd say the chance was 50–50.'

'You've never mentioned that before,' said George, 'you've just thought it up now.'

'Quite right,' said Jos, 'I have. It never occurred to me before, yet it's so very probable.'

'I'd call it convenient,' said George, 'and I despise you for it.'

'All the same, what if it isn't?' pressed Jos.

George clicked her tongue impatiently. 'It's ridiculous to even think like that,' she said, 'and anyway it doesn't make any difference.'

'On the contrary, it makes all the difference if my parenthood is the big obstacle to our going off together.'

'Shut up,' yelled George. 'I wish you'd bloody well stop trying to do a Socrates act and behave like a human being for a minute.'

'We're getting nowhere fast,' said Jos after a short interval during which he reflected that he'd got George on the hop.

'So let's be quiet,' said George sharply.

'Meredith comes out tomorrow. Are you coming with me?'

'No.'

'If I stay, will you tell her right away we want her to leave?'

'No,' said George. She had stopped thinking.

'Remember there's no baby coming with her,' said Jos. 'Are we three going to live indefinitely together?'

George chewed the inside of her cheek with her molars. 'It's so stupid to make bargains,' she said.

'Why, were you thinking of one?' said Jos.

'I'll agree to telling Meredith tomorrow if you will stop the adoption of the baby, or at least get it held up.'

'Done,' said Jos, quickly.

'Then you do think she's yours?' said George, quickly.

'No, though it probably is. I want you, on any terms.'

'Don't you want your daughter for her own sake?' said George.

'No.'

'Then there's not much point in having her.'

'None at all,' said Jos, 'except that it would salve our consciences.'

'So you've got one?' said George, bitterly.

He let that one go. He didn't dare ask if the bargain was still on, nor did he know whether she was going to stay, but he wouldn't ask. The thing to do was to act normally, as though nothing had happened, and assume that when Meredith arrived she would let him tell her the truth, and then leave with him. It was as he imagined the eve of a great battle, so much in doubt because the strength but not the luck of the antagonist was known, nor exactly how he would strike. He felt rather grand, thinking this, and almost made his striking analogy to George, but decided she would not appreciate it.

There was a routine to their evenings, even after ten days, which Jos cherished. They ate about seven, then washed up together, and then sat and read the *Evening Standard* for half an hour, lapsing into a semi-coma of pure indolence afterwards. As dusk came, they lay on the sofa with their feet up and talked until about ten, when they went for a walk round the square, and then straight to bed. They did nothing and went nowhere and saw no one, and wallowed in their smug content. There was nothing quite like being self-sufficient, or sufficient with one other person who was always there. It reduced onlookers to frenzied contempt, larded with unconcealed jealousy.

The evening passed according to pattern. Jos wondered how George could contemplate giving all this up and George wondered what it was all worth anyway, why she should value what amounted to very little. She was doing nothing she didn't do on her own, if you didn't calculate the bed part, which wasn't what made their evenings so happy anyway. Neither spoke, Jos because he was afraid to, and George because she had nothing to say.

Meredith came home in a taxi at three o'clock the next afternoon. She yelled 'George!' at the top of her voice from the pavement outside the house, and when a flustered head was thrust out of the window she roared 'Throw me down some money to pay the taxi.' George retreated and to Jos's disgust ran into the bedroom where she excitedly raked around for something solid enough to throw.

'What's the hurry?' said Jos irritably, 'let her wait.'

'Have you got any silver?'

'No.'

'Then I'll have to go down with this ten shilling note.' Calling 'I'm coming' she ran out of the flat and thundered down the stairs. Jos, watching from the window, saw her hurtle out of the front door to where Meredith was tapping her foot impatiently.

She handed the note over. Meredith gave it to the taximan, who gave her some change, which she put in her pocket. The taxi drove off, and the two of them stood there for a minute. He drew his head in, and walked round the room waiting for them to come in. Somehow, the waiting by himself made it seem as though it was two against one.

They were talking as they came in, George asking eager questions, Meredith slapping her down with her usual terse replies. Awkwardly, he grasped the back of a chair and leant on it as he said 'Hello'. Meredith ignored him.

'I expect you're hungry,' George said to her.

'You bloody well bet I am,' said Meredith.

'I'll go and make you something,' said George.

'No,' said Jos, 'you sit down. She's not that starving. We've got things to say to her that can't wait.'

'For Christ's sake,' said Meredith, staring.

'Jos, please,' said George, flushing an ugly red. 'It can wait.'

'It can't,' said Jos. He grasped George's wrist firmly as she prepared to make off.

'Watch it,' said Meredith, 'she's stronger than you.'

'George and I – ' began Jos.

'You sound like the Queen – mae husband and I,' said Meredith, giggling.

'George and I are in love. We've been living together the last ten days. I want a divorce as quickly as possible,' said Jos. George stopped struggling.'

'Meredith, I didn't mean this to happen,' she began. Already she was crawling.

'Do you think,' said Meredith, 'that you could let her go and make me something to eat now that you've got your pronouncement over? Or is there something else vital to say?'

'We'll adopt the baby,' said Jos, poker-faced.

Meredith laughed till she cried. They stood and watched her, foolishly beginning to smile themselves, the way people do caught up in someone else's hysteria. Nothing more could be said until Meredith had stopped, so they stood waiting in front of her with Jos still holding George by the wrist.

'Oh that's bloody marvellous,' said Meredith at last, 'as if I cared who adopted the brat. I've forgotten about it already.'

'That's beside the point,' said Jos.

'Why tell me then?' said Meredith. 'You made it sound like a great bribe.'

'We just thought you ought to know,' said Jos.

'Ta very much. I wish you luck. George will make a wonderful mother,' said Meredith contemptuously. 'It's her natural role in life though I never thought she would find a willing father.'

There was a pause, distinct and uncomfortable. Jos and George still waited, neither sitting down, while Meredith searched around for a cigarette. 'You get on my nerves,' she said, finding and lighting one. 'For God's sake sit down.'

'We'd like to know,' said Jos.

'Know what?'

'Whether you'll consent to divorcing me as quickly as possible,' said Jos. It was humiliating to have to repeat it.

'Well, naturally,' said Meredith, 'I find the thought of this little love match revolting, but go ahead. I don't know why I married you anyway.'

'Neither do I,' said Jos.

'Forget it,' said Meredith. 'I have.'

George wept openly with happiness and relief, which as Meredith said was very messy. Then she started telling Meredith how wonderful she was, and how she couldn't have behaved like that, so selflessly, in such a spirit of real understanding and friendship. She said she would never forget it, and that she wanted Meredith to go on thinking of them as her closest friends, and anything they could do for her they would do, she only had to ask. Meredith promptly asked for something to eat and George leapt into the kitchen instantly.

It was, Jos reflected, dangerously like old times. Meredith made herself at home, taking her shoes off and sprawling on the sofa where she read a magazine and smoked their cigarettes, while George cooked and presently waited upon her. There was a flatness about her amiable consent to their plans which left a disappointed tinge hanging in the air, yet it was typical. He'd expected violently selfish opposition, but he ought to have known the opposite was complete disinterest. He wanted her out of the flat, quickly.

'When are you leaving?' he said, before George came in.

'That's gratitude,' said Meredith.

'I'm not grateful. Why the hell should I be? Anyway, we won't go into that. I want to know when you're getting out – the sooner the better.'

'You've a bloody cheek,' said Meredith, and raising her voice said, 'George, your darling lover wants to throw me out this minute. I can stay, can't I?'

George was in the room immediately. 'Leave?' she said, 'but you've just come out of hospital. You're not fit to go anywhere. You ought to go straight to bed.'

'There you are,' said Meredith triumphantly.

'I just asked when you planned to go,' said Jos.

'I don't plan to go anywhere at the moment,' said Meredith. 'Actually, I don't really see why I should go at all, do you George? I didn't mind George living here when we were married. Why should she mind me?'

'It's George's flat,' said Jos.

'She wouldn't turn me out, would you, George?' said Meredith confidently.

'No,' said George, and turning to Jos, 'I don't think you realize what Meredith has been through or what we owe her,' she said severely.

Jos groaned and buried his face in his hands, which produced a sarcastic giggle from Meredith. He lay back in his chair and put a cushion over his face, hearing George telling Meredith not to take any notice of him. Through the shifting darkness he heard them chattering, and the clang of knives and forks as George laid the table. This would be the pattern of countless other days, and all he would have of the real George would be the nights in bed. Meredith would never leave and George would never stop debasing herself before her. He didn't want any part of it.

He half thought that he would be the one to end up on the

divan in the sitting room that night, but Meredith took possession of it quite willingly, and peacefully, at about ten o'clock, which saved any argument. She said she'd lie and read for a bit, but she was tired, so George said quickly that she and Jos would go to bed too and give her a bit of peace. Meredith smiled mockingly as they went through into the bedroom and told them to enjoy themselves. George blushed.

Once the bedroom door was closed, Jos felt better. He went over to George and tried to kiss her, but she shook him off.

'What's the matter?' he said.

'Ssh,' she said, 'not so loud,' and pointed to the wall between the two rooms.

'Oh God,' said Jos. 'When we're in the same room as her, we're like strangers, and when we're alone you act as though she was sitting looking at us with a pair of binoculars through the keyhole. That's great.'

'It's just that you must have some tact and consideration,' George said. 'It must be awful for her.'

'It's awful for me,' said Jos.

'What have you got to moan about?' said George, sharply.

'Sharing you with that clever little bitch.'

'Don't be silly. You're not sharing me at all.'

'You've spent all evening talking to her.'

'Well, if you will bury yourself under a cushion and sulk,' said George, 'what do you expect me to do? You were perfectly childish. Meredith is my friend and I'm not going to turn her out for no reason.'

'So she's going to live with us when we're married?' said Jos.

'No. Of course not.'

'When is she going then? The day we get married?'

'I don't know. When she feels strong enough and has found somewhere else.'

'That will be never,' said Jos.

'Look,' said George, 'you spent all last night telling me she wouldn't give us a divorce out of sheer spite. Instead, she agreed right away. Now you say she'll live here forever and ruin our lives, and I don't believe that either. One day, she'll just go.'

'One day I'll fly,' said Jos.

George got into bed and turned away from him, hitching the covers firmly over her shoulders and lying stiffly like a ramrod. Soaked in pessimism, he lay with his hands behind his head, staring into the darkness and counting the days till he left. Nothing could save them. It would all end as suddenly as it had begun. George made no overtures of friendship, so he let her lie, though he knew she was awake too. It was ridiculous that Meredith's placid acceptance of the situation should be the thing to drive them apart. He sighed heavily, and then again. George turned towards him. 'Jonah,' she said, and 'Misery.' She cuddled down beside him.

Jos went back to work the day after Meredith came out of hospital. He was entitled to four more days' holiday, but he thought he would save them, for his honeymoon or something. When he left, Meredith was still in bed and George got quite angry with him when he whistled too loudly. However, he put up with that as good-humouredly as possible and kissed George good-bye.

'Don't forget the baby,' she said.

Jos stared. 'But surely we're not still having it?' he said. 'I mean, now that Meredith's agreed and we're staying here.'

George's face set in obstinate lines of stony calm.

'That doesn't make any difference,' she said. 'Try and ring up or go and see about it in your lunch hour.'

Throughout the morning he pondered on whether he should or he shouldn't, and when he finally decided to try to get his baby back it was a tactical move. He had a shrewd idea that Meredith would not relish the arrival in the flat of her baby, it would push her out quicker than anything else. So he went round to the adoption society's headquarters and announced that he wanted his own baby back, please.

It was two weeks before the baby finally arrived, and that was express service. Jos was tired of signing forms and being interviewed and swearing that he wouldn't change his mind again. He thought it absolute impertinence to screen him so fiercely when it was his child after all, and said as much, many times, very pompously. But George kept him at it and told him off furiously when he said it was all for her, as though the baby was some extravagant present. Meredith said nothing, but smiled derisively when he related the various sagas about his dealings with the society.

They, George and Jos, collected the baby in a taxi. George cradled her tenderly in her arms, while Jos tried to work up some interest.

'Does she look different?' said George.

'About the same,' said Jos. He tried to recognize the tiny creased face and couldn't. 'A bit fatter.'

The taxi driver helped her out. He was discretion itself as he said, 'You'll make a lovely mother, madam.'

'I hope so,' George said.

'Poor little mite,' the driver said. 'It makes you think, don't it?' Jos paid him off hurriedly.

George climbed the stairs carefully. As they reached the flat, the baby began to cry, whining and shrill. Jos hummed loudly.

'It sounds like a circus,' said Meredith.

'Hold her while I heat her bottle,' said George, thrusting the child towards her.

'No thank you,' said Meredith sharply, 'I had enough of that in hospital.'

George plonked her burden into Jos's arms. He stood in the centre of the room, holding the howling cargo. 'Jog her up and down,' shouted George from the kitchen. He jogged. The baby stopped. He stopped, and it cried, so he jogged again, vigorously. 'Must give its innards hell,' he said.

He seemed to be running around the whole evening, obeying George's commands to bring pins, fold that nappy, put this in the bin, let the cot sides down, pull the blanket up, put the light out. Exhausted, he collapsed in a chair. 'Will it sleep all night?' he said hopefully.

'No,' said George, 'she'll wake every four hours for feeds.'

'Oh God,' said Jos, 'let's push the cot in here.' Meredith rustled her newspaper pointedly. 'Sorry,' he said, 'I forgot we couldn't do that. It's mother wouldn't like it.'

'We must choose a name,' said George. She'd produced yet another needleful of baby knitting from somewhere.

'All yours,' said Jos, grandly.

'It's so important,' said George. 'Look at my awful name. What about Jane? It's a nice, steady name and you can't mess it up.'

'Fine,' said Jos. 'Jane it is.'

'Or Anne,' said George.

'Might as well call a child "the" if you're going to call it Anne,' said Jos. 'Jane will do.'

'Jane what?' said George. 'Jane Elizabeth?'

'Fine,' said Jos.

'Jane Elizabeth Jones. Jane Jones – oh no Jos, that doesn't sound right. Jane Jones sounds like a nursery rhyme.'

'Elizabeth, then,' said Jos, wearily.

'But she might get called Liz.'

'I like Liz.'

'Or Betty.' George paused in the middle of a line. 'What about Tanya.'

'Christ,' said Meredith, and threw down her paper.

'None of your business,' said Jos, quickly.

'Don't you like Tanya, Meredith?' said George anxiously. 'Maybe Tanya Jones does sound a bit far fetched. What names do you like?'

'It doesn't matter what she likes,' said Jos, 'you're choosing the name.'

'I don't give a damn,' said Meredith. 'You can call it what you like, only for God's sake hurry up about it because it's driving me mad.'

'You don't have to stay,' said Jos.

She picked up the paper again and disappeared stoically behind it.

Maliciously, Jos swallowed his own boredom and drew George out on the name game endlessly. They went through every name they could both lay their tongues on, with Jos apparently agreeing and then at the last minute withdrawing his enthusiasm. Meredith's paper twitched uncontrollably. When they'd gone back to discussing the merits and demerits of Jane for the fourth time, she got up.

'Going out?' said Jos gaily. For answer, Meredith grabbed her coat from behind the door and struggled into it. She slammed out of the flat and woke the still unnamed child.

'Do you think she's angry?' said George, already on her feet to rush to the cot.

'I hope so,' said Jos. 'Anyway, she's out, gone, vamoosed. Do you realize this is the first time we've been really alone since she came back? I feel like double locking the door.'

'Don't be silly,' said George, and began to pick the baby up.

'You'll spoil that child,' said Jos sternly.

'Do you think so?' said George, withdrawing her arms.

'Certainly – picking it up every time it cries.' He watched George hover uncertainly over the cot, until a frenzied howl decided her and she picked the baby up and cradled it in her arms.

'Doesn't it make any difference?' he said.

'What?'

'That it's not yours. I don't see how you can love it so much.'

George didn't answer.

'I'm jealous,' he said. 'Meredith's gone and I wanted you all to myself.'

'You can have me, when she's asleep.'

He waited dutifully until the sniffling bundle had been put back in the cot, and then led George eagerly to the sofa and his arms. He kissed her warmly and she responded.

'What about Sara, without an "h"?' she said in his ear.

'Definitely,' said Jos, 'definitely Sara without an "h". Perfect. That's settled then. Don't say a word. It's decided.'

Meredith went round the square twice at a gallop. She didn't know why she hadn't smacked both their smug faces. She should have put her foot down and stopped them getting the baby, instead of being too idle and short-sighted to see that it mattered. Already, it was getting her down. The Sister would have said she was suffering from delayed guilt feelings, but that wasn't true at all. She didn't care about the baby, she really didn't, it was those two she hated. They behaved as though they were in some private world, all sugar and spice and all things nice. She despised them and their cosiness. She hadn't thought Jos could stoop so low.

They probably wouldn't give her her job back. It was six months since she'd worked and there were scores of first violinists all ready to murder each other to get a place in an established orchestra. If she couldn't get in, there was nothing else she wanted to do, much. She reminded herself that she had no money, that she hadn't had any for a long time. Grimly, she stopped walking and leant against a pillar box. She was furious with herself for getting so annoyed and now so worried. Jos would realize he had scored and would try again. He wanted her out of the flat, but she wasn't going to go. Or should she? If she deliberately stayed just to spite them, she might regret it. It might mean good-bye to detachment. She'd lose her temper more often, react all the time to the remarks Jos would put in her way. She was better out of it, not caring, with nothing and no one to make her sorry or glad or annoyed. Above it all, that's what she must strive to stay.

There was no time like the present. All her clothes were in the flat, but she could collect them some time. She could hire or borrow or steal a violin, until she was stable enough to collect her own. She felt inside her pockets and found fourteen shillings and three halfpence, the change from the pound George had given her to get cigarettes. It would do to start her off. She turned her back on the square and ran to catch a bus.

Chapter Seven

The bank looked quiet. The doors, which opened cornerwise on to the street, were open to let in the early September sunshine, and the shafts of light streamed across the brown floor to the deeper brown of the long, heavy counter. There was the rustle of notes as the cashier counted them out for the solitary customer, stopping at every fifth one to select another pile. He, and all the five men behind the counter, wore dark suits and white shirts and all their heads looked as though they had been brushed by their mothers. That was the front line. Behind them were three other men and a girl, all equally immaculate in a dull, unnoticeable way. Except for Jos.

Jos sat at the end of the rear brigade at a small table. It was his job to check the bank statements being sent out, and enclose them with all the current cheques cashed. He put the whole lot into a large envelope, addressed it, and passed it on for posting. Sometimes he was called upon to stand in for one of the front line men, which he resented. Sitting at his little table he acquired such a deep feeling of sloth that the physical task of getting from one place to another exhausted him. He sat there, trance-like, day after day, looking through the doors and breaking the stillness with the clatter of his pen inside the pot.

There were tea breaks. Then he would go into the room at the back among all the unsubdued typists and drink his tea. He nearly always went back before he had to, into the calm of the 'shop front'. At lunchtime, he went to a pub and had a glass of bitter and a nosh of shepherd's pie, or two sausages and half a tomato. Afterwards, he went for a walk in a small nearby park, or if it was wet he went round the basement of Gamages looking at things. No one ever went with him. He realized it was his own fault that he'd made no friend at the bank, but that was the way he'd wanted it. All the men of his age were married and had children and lived at Pinner or Beckenham. He told himself he had nothing in common with them, except everything.

Just when he would leave he didn't exactly know, but meanwhile he struggled to keep his individuality. He wore pale blue button-down shirts and high-necked jackets and straight, narrow ties. His hair was shining and sleek, but he had adopted a Beatles' style which made everyone look twice to see if it was dirty. His trousers were very narrow and his shoes elegant. He was very well dressed, if with little variety because he hadn't much money. With the band, he hadn't been nearly so particular about his clothes, although he was on view much more then.

Sometimes he thought that after all it would be foolish to simply get up and go, which was what he had kept at the back of his mind from the day he started. He liked the quiet and the calm – he must do, or he wouldn't resent any intrusion so much. What better than gently drifting life away in such a civilized manner? He had no ambitions, he was untroubled by materialistic greed. The reason, he concluded after many quiet afternoons listening to the flies buzz through the door, was that he was a hedonist. The bank wasn't positive, active pleasure. It was enjoyable calm, as different from pleasure as contentment from ecstasy. Nothing there made him excited or worried, he didn't look forward to going there, one day was uneventfully like the last. There were no kicks.

None of this would have mattered if life outside the bank had been different. Most people were bored by their jobs, he realized that, but they made up for it outside. Life began at 5.30 p.m. Jos was beginning to feel that for him it ended. At 5.30 p.m. he went home to George and the baby, finally named Sara. There, the bank calm was missing but the monotony redoubled. They never went out, because George didn't approve of baby sitters. They didn't watch tele because they couldn't afford it. They didn't have friends in because they hadn't any. They didn't make love very often, because George was tired. Altogether, it was deadly.

For one short week, it had been idyllic. Thinking this, Jos told himself he lied in his teeth. It had never been idyllic. The removal of Meredith, for which he had schemed and longed, was simply followed by a short period of relief and reaction. He had George all to himself and that was supposed to be what mattered. Only, of course, he didn't have her to himself any more than he had done with Meredith around. There was Sara to contend with, forever needing to be fed and changed and rocked to sleep. She seemed to know when he came home and howled in greeting as he entered the front, downstairs door.

Yet it wasn't all Sara's fault. George was too ready and willing to slave over her. Sometimes she would actually go to see if she needed changing when the baby was blissfully asleep, or go on trying to force milk down her throat long after it was apparent that she'd had enough. At night George lay awake listening for her cry, and when she allowed him to make love she was abstracted and tense. Once, she had made him break off in the middle so that she could go to Sara.

They hadn't exactly stopped talking. After supper, and if Sara had gone off to sleep and George had stopped clearing up the baby debris that seemed to accumulate each day, they still sat on the sofa each night and talked. George talked. She asked him where Sara was going to go to school. He said whatever school happened to be at the end of the street they were living in when she was five. George said he couldn't mean a State school and he said none other and then they argued until George cried because she said he didn't care what happened to his daughter. Alternatively, she asked him when he thought Sara should be punished and how, and when he said he'd know when the occasion arose, she wanted him to tell her how *she* would know. She worried about Sara's height and looks, whether she would be tall and ugly like her. Jos said he didn't see why Sara should bear any resemblance to her, as she wasn't her mother, apart from the fact that she wasn't tall and ugly anyway. George cried for a solid hour.

There was one other topic of conversation apart from Sara: George's sterility. She hadn't become pregnant. Jos replied, rather bitterly, that he wasn't surprised as surely she'd noticed she'd been slightly nun-like recently. George said that didn't explain it, they'd made love enough times for her to have been pregnant if she was normal. She wanted to know what she should do about it, whether she, or both of them, should go to see a doctor, or go to a clinic, or what they should do. Jos said, emphatically, that considering their relationship was exactly three months old any doctor would think them crackers. George lapsed into a frustrated silence, leaving Jos to shudder with horror at the thought of another baby.

Actually, they had one faithful visitor in Peg, whom Jos could well have done without. She came up about eight in the evening, every Tuesday and Thursday when she didn't have any classes. Usually, she brought her rug-making tools and sat pulling pieces of rag about in a slow, obsessed way. Her greeting every night was, 'I just thought I'd come and pay my respects to the baby.' George would usher her in and they both bent over the cot for a minute's silence. Should Sara be crying, Peg didn't offer to hold her, but sat and shook her head and said, 'There's a child that needs loving.'

On those evenings, Jos was driven to near suicide. Peg was the audience, the stooge, that George needed. She was willing to debate endlessly not only education and punishment as related to Sara, but also whether her complexion was good or bad, whether she was constipated, whether she should be put on to mixed feeding then, or later, or never. George had the edge in these interchanges because she had possession of Sara, but Peg's comments as an outsider had all the weight of an impartial observer and they drove George frantic. Peg had only to say that her cousin's baby was Sara's age but twice her weight for George to be convinced Sara was desperately ill. She would ask Peg if she thought Sara was being fed properly and go into exact details of what she was given. Peg would consider, purse her lips, and say it wasn't for her to say. George would beg her to say, but Peg knew her advantage and held silently on to it. Pronouncement might prove her wrong, discretion never could.

Jos felt all this couldn't go on, but he knew it would. Like the bank, inevitably and imperceptibly, his home life would take on an immovable pattern. Come home, take his coat off, eat, help to wash up, help to put Sara to sleep, read the paper, fall into a doze listening to George, go to bed. There wasn't even an open door to gaze at and imagine himself walking through. At the bank, no one would much care or be affected by his disappearance, but at home the implications of desertion were terrible.

At least, that was what he thought before he tried to make George see what she was doing to him.

'Let's go out,' he said one evening.

'Don't be silly,' said George, 'you know perfectly well we can't leave Sara.'

'Peg could baby sit,' he said.

'I don't want her to,' said George.

'In fact you'd rather stay here with Sara, who's asleep, than go out with me,' he said.

'Yes. I don't know why you want to go out.'

'Because I'm bored,' he said.

'You want to grow up,' George said.

'In this atmosphere,' he said, 'my growth is stunted.'

'Go by yourself,' George said, 'I don't mind.'

'Fine,' he said, and went.

It wasn't that he had scruples of conscience. George had said she was perfectly happy staying in, it wasn't as though she was being a martyr. He knew she really did prefer to stay in, that was what angered him. She didn't need his companionship, she didn't want to talk to him or do anything with him more than she wanted to be with Sara. There was no closeness, no unity at all. It was as if she had put the clock back a hundred years, when a man would rightly expect his wife to stay at home, obsessed by her children and household cares, while he pursued his own pastimes. He might as well be 'Mr Jones' to her. He didn't want to develop his own amusements in which she had no part. He hated to think of the pubs he could go to and form a drinking circle of acquaintances, or the band he could join again and play for in the evenings. He wanted George, and if he couldn't have her all the time, he didn't want her as a drudge and housewife and mother.

She wasn't his wife anyway. Since Meredith had walked out, they hadn't seen her, though she had sent them an address and asked them to forward all her belongings without mentioning the means of transport or who was going to pay for it. Jos had refused to send anything unless she sent the money. Instead, a man had turned up in a mini van one evening saying Meredith had asked him to collect all her things. They were only too pleased to get rid of them. It meant, however, that contact wasn't renewed so the question of the divorce hung fire, and until he was divorced he couldn't marry George.

The angle that worried her was Sara's opinion, and what people might think later if they knew her father lived with a woman who wasn't his wife or her mother.

'It will be years before that becomes a problem,' Jos said.

'I don't know,' George said, 'it might take years to get divorced.'

'Not with Meredith's co-operation,' Jos said.

'Then get it,' said George.

'Why?'

George didn't pretend to misunderstand. 'Don't you want to marry me?'

'Not particularly,' Jos said abruptly.

'You've changed,' George said.

'You mean you have.'

She didn't deny it. She picked up Sara defensively, as though that were explanation enough.

'I don't like marriage,' Jos said, 'not marriage with children.'

'Child,' George said.

'Child, then. You don't love me, except as Sara's father. You couldn't be less interested in me.'

'I know,' said George. 'I can't help it.'

If he left her, he would be the only one hurt. He thought wildly of dumping Sara in a river, to see if that would bring George back, but it wasn't likely to. She would just carry on as usual, only thinking instead about her own child she so desperately wanted. And yet he was reluctant to go. She had no money, since she'd given up her classes when Sara arrived. He supposed her family would keep her, but there was a chance they might not. No one would marry her, and Sara would go away when she grew up. Furthermore, George would have no legal right to the baby, and that would haunt her.

He remembered how he had married Meredith out of a sense of duty, and where that had landed him. He could stay with George with better justification, because he loved her, but for his own future it would be as catastrophic as marrying Meredith, if he wanted a future.

Almost as a test, he left the bank. It wasn't even the lure of the sun shafts coming through the door that drew him out, because it was raining and the doors were tight closed. He could hear the rain beating on the glass panels as he sat at his desk and felt his pay packet still square and firm, in his pocket. Winter's coming, poor Jos is a' cold, he chanted, and leaving his desk got up, passed through the front line and tugging the doors open walked through them without so much, sir, as a by-your-leave.

It seemed very important to get home as quickly as possible, as though coming on George unexpectedly would give him some miraculous power over her. He ran for a bus, leapt on it, and sat in the nearest seat to the door to get off all the quicker when it got to his stop. He was off, straight into a puddle, before the bus had really slowed down, and as he ran down the road into the square his wet shoe and sock squelched and clung unpleasantly to his foot. By the time he reached the outside door of the house, he was soaked. He hammered frantically with the knocker and only when no one answered, stopped to search for his key. He'd forgotten it. There was no one in the building. Furious, he huddled into the door under the mere six inches of overhanging porch.

The whole square was empty and desolate, the trees in the middle thin, mean streaks stripped of their leaves which lay in drenched but bright piles all round them. He left the inadequate shelter of the doorway and suddenly not caring about the rain he walked slowly over to the trees. The gate to the garden was closed, as usual. He vaulted over it and on to the small triangle of glowing grass. He bent down and picked up three of the biggest and most vivid leaves, orange, orangey yellow, and red, and stuck them in his lapel where they flattened themselves out against the wet tweed. Then he leant against the railings and waited for George, with his back to the trees he had wanted to reach and touch.

She looked about forty. She looked like a suburban housewife loaded down with pounds of stewing steak and the washing for the launderette. It was her huddled, drooping walk, hands clutching the handle of the pram firmly, more than the old leather coat strapped tightly round her waist. She had wellingtons on, short ones, and breasted every puddle dauntlessly. On top of the pram was a bag covered with a plastic mack. The pram cover was securely hooked on to the hood, but even then she seemed worried that Sara would get wet and kept peering anxiously at her, pushing the pram with one hand and walking along beside it so as not to lose time.

She didn't see him even though she passed quite close. Her head-square, pulled unbecomingly low on her forehead, acted as blinkers do to a horse.

'Whoa there,' he said, as she came level with him.

She stopped and looked back, pushing a long strand of wet hair back under cover.

'I'm soaked,' she said.

'So am I,' he said.

She began to move on. He stayed where he was, just to disconcert her, and watched her dash across the road, the pram sticking momentarily on the kerb, and up to the door. She fumbled for the key, opened the door, and lugged the pram through it. For a few minutes, she disappeared, then he saw her at the window beckoning impatiently. He waved cheerfully, and pulling the leaves out of his lapel brandished them above his head. Taking his time, he climbed back over the railings and dawdled into the house. As he climbed the stairs, he took off his streaming jacket, and trailed it behind him, hearing with satisfaction the wet sploshes as it bumped on each stair.

The flat was full of steam, rising in clouds from a clothes horse draped with nappies in front of the electric fire. All the windows were misted over. He went towards them, and rubbed a hole clear in the corner pane so that he could look out on to the square.

'You'd better get out of those wet clothes,' George said.

Jos started taking them off, flinging them into the corner one by one. When he was naked, he went across to the fire and took the clothes horse away so that he could get warm. He stood with his hands behind his back and beamed at her.

'I suppose you've left the bank,' she said.

'Correct,' he said.

'I'm not surprised,' she said dully.

'Oh go on, be surprised,' he begged. 'I'd like to surprise you.'

'Did you get your pay before you left?' she asked.

'Yes.'

'Thank God for that,' she said. 'I wouldn't have been a bit surprised if you'd been too high and mighty to think about that.'

'So you are surprised,' he said. 'Hurrah.'

'Oh shut up,' she said. 'I suppose you think you've done your bit actually working for ten whole months at a steady job.'

'Well, I do rather,' he said.

'And now you're just going to sit around and wait for money to arrive from heaven.'

'I haven't actually thought what I'm going to do,' he said.

'It amazes me.' George stopped, her voice was shaking. 'It amazes me how a man with your responsibilities can behave the way you do.'

'You're a shrew,' Jos said. 'I would never have thought it possible, but you've turned into a first class shrew and it doesn't become you.'

'Should I be pleased you've given up your job?' she said bitterly.

'Yes,' he said, 'you once told me money didn't matter and said you didn't see why I should have to work in a bank just for the sake of getting it. You said I should stick to music at all costs.'

'Things have changed,' she said, 'the circumstances were quite different then.'

'Apparently,' he said.

George abruptly grabbed the clothes horse. 'I'd like to put these back,' she said, 'if you've finished.'

'I'm entitled to warm my arse as long as I like,' said Jos, smiling benignly. 'You may put them to one side.'

She snatched a wet nappy and hit him with it. The sharp, knife-like edge left a long red mark across his chest. He picked up the clothes horse and held it in front of himself like a shield, shouting encouragement to her until she had torn all the nappies off and he was left with the empty framework. He was just beginning to relish the approaching unarmed combat, when she suddenly sat down and started to cry.

'Oh Christ,' he said, in disgust.

She went on howling. Quietly, he set the horse up and arranged the nappies neatly on it in front of the fire, then, whistling, he went into the bathroom and ran a hot bath.

George was still bawling as he stepped into it and lay back, balancing his toes in between the taps. He had to listen carefully to hear her above the noise of the hot water tank gurgling and choking above him. When that noise stopped, he heard the sniffs that meant she had nearly finished. Contentedly, he smiled, and told himself he shouldn't hold it against her that she cried so much, so often, and for so little. It was a reflex reaction. Some people bit their nails, or smoked, she cried. Her cries had grades too, according to the amount and quality of emotion involved.

After his bath, he dressed in his most casual clothes and settled down to read the paper. He didn't speak, but kept smiling at George so that she would have no cause to think there was any row as far as he was concerned. Sara seemed very quiet. The only one making any noise was George as she stalked backwards and forwards doing her housework. When she'd brushed and patted everything in sight, she went into the kitchen and closed the door. Jos reached for the telephone and the directory and hoped she wouldn't hear.

The rain stopped at twelve o'clock and a thin sun came straggling through the still threatening clouds. George made them both an omelette, which Jos ate with relish, humming in between forkfuls.

'I'm going to take Sara for a walk,' he said.

'Where? You don't usually take her out,' said George suspiciously.

'No, I don't, do I?' said Jos politely, 'but then I don't usually have all day to myself.'

He waited, but George could hardly object.

'Are you coming?' he said, when he was ready.

'No,' she said. 'I'll take the opportunity to really clean the bedroom out.'

'What a marvellous idea,' Jos said. 'You do that.'

She came with him as far as the outside door, still fussing over the pram.

'Don't put the hood down,' she said, 'there's a cold wind.'

'I wouldn't dream of it,' Jos said.

'You won't leave her outside a shop or anything, will you?' George said.

'Her highness will be attended every waking or sleeping moment,' Jos promised.

'How long will you be?'

'Not long. You get cracking on that bedroom.'

He was aware that she was watching as he wheeled the chariot slowly along the square with the utmost decorum.

In half an hour, he was back. The rain was still holding off and more blue sky appeared every second from nowhere. He felt like going on the river.

George wheeled round from the drawer she was tidying as he came into the flat.

'You've hardly been out,' she said accusingly. 'What's the matter? There's nothing wrong with Sara is there?'

'Nothing,' said Jos. 'Sara is blooming. I left her in hands even more experienced and loving than yours.'

'You left her – whatever do you mean?' said George, feeling suddenly sick and faint.

'I took her to a nursery and said could they look after her for a few hours because my wife was very ill and I had to take her to hospital.'

'You liar!'

'I know,' said Jos smiling. 'I probably needn't have said that but I thought it might make things easier.'

'I'm not ill. I don't want to be rid of her – if I'd known you were just dumping her somewhere instead of pretending you wanted to take her for a walk, I'd never have let her out of the flat.'

'Well, she's there now,' said Jos, 'so you might as well make the most of it. I thought we'd go on the river – sail to Greenwich or somewhere. What do you think?'

'I think you're the most selfish, unfeeling bastard that ever walked this earth,' said George.

Jos let the pose of the last few hours slip off his shoulders. He stopped smiling and concentrating on being jaunty, and let her see how tired and defeated he was, before he could trust himself to speak.

'It's only one afternoon George,' he pleaded. 'I'm miserable and upset. You don't seem to love me, I can't stand my job any more. I need just one afternoon alone with you.' She shrugged and turned away. 'Please,' he said, 'even if you think I'm being melodramatic. I don't have to go down on my knees and beg you, do I?'

'No,' said George, 'you don't. I'll come, just to show you that it won't do any good. I won't enjoy it one bit either.'

He was about to make a sarcastic rejoinder, or tell her in that case she could go to hell and he'd spend the afternoon packing instead. But he swallowed his anger, and told himself it was all this he had to overcome in one short afternoon.

They took a bus down to the Embankment and walked along to Westminster Bridge. There was a boat sailing to Greenwich in fifteen minutes, for which Jos bought two return tickets. He felt nervous and didn't know what to suggest to put in the time, but luckily the boat was already tied up there and they clambered on board and took seats in the front part. George was sullen and sat huddled into her coat as though the day was much colder than it really was.

By the time the boat left, it was nearly full. Comfortably so, no one was squashed and there was plenty of room to put raincoats and bags and feet. Jos wondered where everyone had come from because none of them looked like tourists. There was not a camera in sight, nor a map. They must all have their own private, desperate reasons for sailing to Greenwich on a doubtful, late September Wednesday afternoon. Seized with a sense of excitement, he twisted in his seat to look back at Big Ben as the boat swung round into the river and the engines chugged noisily into action. By the time he saw Big Ben again, in two hours' time, he promised himself that all would be decided, and almost said it aloud to George, as though it was only fair to warn her that her fate hung in the balance. Solemnly, he turned in his seat and settled down instead, to wait.

There was a guide of sorts on the boat, with a good line in quick and quite witty patter which Jos enjoyed very much. He swung his eyes dutifully from one side of the river to the other as the various landmarks were pointed out, and laughed heartily at all the inevitable quips. George visibly winced, and stared straight ahead, ignoring both Jos and the guide. She wished it would rain, but the sun grew stronger and so did the wind and really by the time they were level with the Tower it was a beautiful afternoon.

'You've got to have a heartache when you fa-all in luv,' sang Jos, and continued the rest of the song in a strong hum.

'You don't sound as though you've got much heartache,' said George sourly.

'Oh but I have,' said Jos. 'It really hurts.'

'Don't be facetious,' snapped George.

'I mean it. Why else should I take such bold and desperate steps to win you all over again?'

'You just wanted an afternoon out,' said George.

'I could have gone on my own.'

'You don't like being on your own.'

'I've been getting used to it recently,' said Jos. She didn't reply. 'Admit you're enjoying yourself,' he said.

'I couldn't,' said George, 'because I'm not. I'm more miserable than you.'

'Why?' said Jos. 'You've got a man who loves you and a baby

you adore. You once said that was all you wanted, especially the first bit.'

'I don't think I love you any more,' said George quietly. 'I want to, but nothing happens.'

Jos cleared his throat. 'You've been cooped up too much with Sara,' he said.

'I want to be,' said George.

'Do you want me to leave you then?' said Jos.

'I don't know. How would we live?'

He tried to keep his voice steady and practical. 'You could put Sara in a nursery and go on with your dancing classes. Or your mother might look after her.'

'She needs a father,' said George.

He couldn't say any more. All anyone wanted to use him for was a father. He vowed that as long as he lived he would take good care never to sire another child for bloodthirsty women to devour. Meredith had had the right idea when she had Sara adopted – there were people who loved children and people who didn't and he and she belonged to the latter category. There was no such thing as a natural instinct. He thought he wouldn't mind being dead. He wouldn't commit suicide or anything, but if it just so happened that he was killed he wouldn't mind. Not that he didn't like being alive, but there were pros and cons for both states. Anyway, he didn't have to wait to see Big Ben again to know that his way was clear. He was finished with duty and responsibility, he'd just go quietly off that evening.

It seemed silly to be stuck in the middle of the river with her after deciding that. He got up and walked round the boat to the other end and stood leaning against the rail. When they got to Greenwich, he'd give her a return ticket and the address of the nursery where he'd left Sara, and then he'd go back to the flat by tube or bus and collect his things.

He walked round to her end again as the boat drew up alongside the quay, and followed her off.

'Your return ticket,' he said, holding it out.

'Why, aren't you going back with me?' she said.

'There doesn't seem much point, does there?' he said. 'I mean, you've proved your case.'

'Right,' she said, 'thanks. Will I see you back at the flat?'

'Probably,' he said.

He turned and went off, and out through the landing stage gates, and then right along the river walk. When he came to a seat, he sat down, and watched the boat he'd just come on loading up to go back. George had got straight back on it, and sat in the same seat. She looked the picture of misery and all the old pity, which was once the only emotion he'd felt for her, came back. She was such a stupid, silly bitch. Once she'd been Meredith's catspaw, making herself ill with jealousy and the conviction that she was ugly and useless and doomed to a dreary life, and now she was Sara's. It was as though she had a talent for martyrdom. All her troubles this time were entirely of her own making. He got worked up thinking about it, and wanted to stretch his arms out over the path and docks that separated them and shake her hard.

He jumped on to the boat just as it was moving off. The captain spent five minutes telling him what a bloody fool he was, and he agreed unreservedly.

'Hello,' he said to George, 'you're very like a girl I used to know. In fact, I once took her for a sail on this boat, only it was the other way – Westminster to Greenwich.'

'Why did you get back on?' George said.

'She was quite an attractive girl really,' Jos said, 'except that she would go around looking suicidal all the time and towards the end of me knowing her she never bothered to comb her hair or anything. She was very sweet and kind and loving too, do anything for anybody, but she had one big fault.'

'You should have stayed in Greenwich,' George said.

'She kept imagining that she had to do things when really she didn't have to do them at all,' said Jos. 'She made herself unhappy when she had everything she could possibly want. She worried herself sick about nothing and forgot that life was quite simple. The basic trouble was an over-active conscience and an inability to take life as it came.'

George got up and moved. He followed her. 'That was a good idea,' he said, 'there's a much better view from this side.'

'Go away,' she said, 'or I'll cry.'

'Really?' Jos said. 'I've never seen you cry. How very peculiar. You mean salt tears will actually run down your cheeks? Now the cause of crying is an excess of something to somewhere, I've forgotten the technicalities. My God, yes, how extraordinary,' he said, putting up a finger, and wiping one tear gently down her cheek, 'tears. Have you thought about patenting them? Shall I cry? I'm trying, but it's very difficult. I don't think I've cried since I fell off the seat of my bike on to the crossbar when I was eight. Can't you teach me? I mean, it must be so very useful being able to cry.' George stopped crying and closed her eyes. 'You've stopped,' he said, 'was it wearing you out too much? What have you got your eyes closed for? Is the pain too great to bear? Heh, fat face, I'm talking to you.' She moved away again, and he followed. 'That's dangerous,' he said, 'you don't want to be waltzing round ships with your eyes closed. Oh, I see, you're maintaining a dignified silence. There's nothing like a bit of dignity for putting a chap in his place. It's really making me shrivel up inside, I can tell you. I'm going all hot and cold with the unbearable humiliation.'

George opened her eyes and looked round for a ladies, but it was a small boat and there wasn't one.

'Do you want to go to the lavatory?' Jos said. 'Forgive me for being crude, but I know how it is. I've always had a weak bladder. I think it was something to do with my early training. Do you know that my mother used to lift all three of us out of bed twice during the night and make us use the pot even if we didn't want to? It was so that we wouldn't wet the sheets. Even now my recurrent nightmare when I'm in a strange house is that I can't find the lavatory. Shall I go and ask the guide if he has his own private one that you could use? I'll do that – won't be a minute.'

'Jos – don't dare,' said George.

'You've spoken. I'll have to sit down, the relief has made my knees go all funny. I was afraid the suppression of emotion coupled with the suppression of urine would paralyse your vocal chords.'

'I'm not really laughing,' George said. The corners of her mouth twitched and her cheeks ached.

'I'm sure you're not,' said Jos. 'You can trust me. Even in the face of violent contortions and strange noises produced from the throat I won't think you're laughing. Other people might, but I won't. I'm not easily fooled. I can see through what other people think is a laugh just like that.' He tried to click his fingers. 'That was meant to be my fingers clicking, only I used my tongue because I can't click my fingers. I'm a ventriloquist actually, I've been taking people in for years. I don't know why I can't click them, I'm like Peter Pan, he couldn't click his you know. It can be very embarrassing.' She was laughing. He bent forward and kissed her and put his arm round her. 'For God's sake make me shut up,' he said. 'I'm shattered.'

George smiled at him uncertainly, and put her hand lightly over his mouth.

'I don't know what makes me behave so stupidly,' she said. 'I'm sorry. It's all my fault.'

Jos firmly knocked aside her hand. 'I can stand anything,' he said, 'except abject apologies. We'll both just shut up.'

They sat close together through what remained of the sail. Jos didn't quite know what he had achieved, if anything, nor where they went from this truce, but he wasn't going to ask. He'd done too much asking, it only encouraged a whole lot of self-analysis that didn't do anyone any good. If they enjoyed fifteen minutes on the river and went home together, that was something to be grateful for.

The wind was blowing into their faces. Jos closed his eyes, and held his face up and back to feel the cold gust. It ought to iron out his worries, like a facial. He tried to concentrate on just feeling and not thinking, but it didn't quite work. His head ached and his eyes felt tight and strained. He shivered.

At half past ten that night, Jos ceremoniously finished packing the large holdall that held all his belongings with ease. There was

147

an old travel tag on it saying 'Aer Lingus', commemorating the one and only time he'd been out of the country. It gave him the idea that he might go to Ireland. He put on his raincoat, lifted the bag up and walked into the sitting room where George was absorbed in feeding Sara. She didn't look up. He pulled out the pay packet which was still in his jacket pocket, and drawing out five pounds, put the other ten on the table.

'I won't come back,' he said, 'but in case you ever want me, you can get me Poste Restante at the post office in Holborn. I'll call there once a week and if I ever get a permanent address I'll let you have it. I'll send you some money every week so don't worry too much. Keep Sara's nose clean and don't take her dear father's name in vain.' He picked up the bag. There was no risk this time of a repeat performance of the afternoon. 'Good-bye, George.' He opened the door as Peg lifted her hand to knock on it.

'I was just going to knock,' she said, 'isn't that funny.'

'I'm splitting my sides,' Jos said. 'Excuse me, I was just leaving.'

'Is George in?' said Peg.

'Naturally,' Jos said. 'Where else would she be at the witching hour? She's all yours, my dear Peg. There you are,' he gestured through the open door, 'a most touching scene, mother with child. And now, if you'll stand aside madam.'

'Are you going out?' said Peg, obeying.

'With your usual brilliance,' said Jos, 'you've penetrated my feeble attempt to disguise my movements. I *am* going out, never more to darken this door. George will make your ears tingle telling you all about it.'

'You're not going on holiday are you?' said Peg, looking at the bag.

'Yes,' said Jos, feeling his patience coming to an end.

'At this time of the year?' said Peg. 'The clocks will be going back soon.'

'I'm going with them,' said Jos, wearily.

'That doesn't make sense.'

'No.' He stepped past her and went down the stairs, closing the outside door quietly behind him.

There were a lot of small things to be done. First, he went to Euston Station and left his bag in the left luggage. Then he rang up a friend he hadn't contacted since he'd married Meredith and asked if he could put him up for a few nights. The friend said no. He went to the nearest Y.M.C.A. and booked in there. By this time it was after eleven, so he went back to the station and had a cup of coffee and a wash and brush-up while he debated whether to spend his five pounds on a ticket somewhere. He decided that would be a waste of five pounds. He'd try to get a job with a band the next day, and if he couldn't, then he would go home to Derby, and recuperate for a few months. He knew, as he made his mind up, that with that alternative as an incentive, he'd land something the next day. He'd live from hand to mouth until he found a team to shack up with, and he'd be as lonely and miserable as hell in the process. He felt cheerful and cocky for the first time in weeks.

'Has he left you?' said Peg, solemnly.

'Yes,' said George.

'Why?'

'He was fed up.'

'Huh,' grunted Peg, 'he'd reason to be fed up, I don't think. What did he have to be fed up about?'

'Quite a lot,' said George.

'You were too soft with him,' said Peg. 'You let him take advantage of you. He took advantage of Meredith and then of you. He shouldn't be allowed to get away with it.'

George sat still, tilting the bottle up so that it trickled more easily into Sara's mouth.

'Did you quarrel?' said Peg, greedily.

'Not exactly,' said George.

'I thought I saw you going out this lunch time. You didn't see me. I was coming out of the library and you passed me. It was about half past one.'

'Yes, that's right,' said George.

'You didn't have Sara with you,' said Peg, 'you didn't leave her on her own did you?'

'No,' said George.

'Where was she then?'

George sighed. It would be much easier and quicker to satisfy Peg's horrible curiosity in one rush, but she had neither the energy to do that nor to tell her to mind her own business and throw her out.

'At the nursery down the road,' she said.

'You put her in a nursery?' said Peg, scandalized.

'Jos did.'

'Why?'

'He wanted to take me out for the afternoon.'

'Where did you go?'

'Greenwich. On the river.'

'Was it nice?' said Peg. 'Did you enjoy it? I don't know how you could, knowing Sara was in a nursery.'

'Yes, I did,' said George. 'We had a good time.'

'What's he left you for then?' said Peg.

'He was fed up,' said George.

'After a nice afternoon out?' said Peg. George remained stoically silent. 'How did he come to be off work anyway?' said Peg. 'It's Wednesday.'

'He left this morning,' said George.

'You mean he was sacked?'

'No, he left. He was fed up.'

'Well,' said Peg, 'that beats the band. What right had he to be fed up with the bank? I'd like to know what the bank thought of him.'

Sara was fed. George held her on her shoulder until she brought her wind up and then went to lay her in the cot. Peg went on sitting there till she came back.

'What will you do?' she said.

'I don't know,' said George. 'Work.'

'Will you keep Sarah?'

'Of course.'

'She's not yours,' said Peg.

'No, I know. But her parents won't ever want her.'

'I don't see why you should keep her,' said Peg.

'Don't you?' said George, distantly. She wished Peg would go. 'I'm going to bed now,' she said.

'Do you want me to stay with you?' said Peg, eagerly. 'I could bring my nightie up in a jiffy.'

'No thank you,' said George. 'Good night.'

She turned and went into the bedroom, leaving the aggrieved Peg to see herself out.

Chapter Eight

George woke up when it was still dark. Automatically, she groped for the cot and bent over it, but the baby was sleeping and making no sound. She got back into bed and pulled the covers up to her neck, staring round the room at the objects which took shape as her eyes grew accustomed to the gloom. The bed felt vast. She stretched out her arms on either side into cold nothingness, and drew them quickly in again to the warmth of her body. She wondered when Sara would be big enough to sleep with her.

Turning on her side, she put her left arm behind her back and curved the other round her head, and pulled her right knee as high as she could. She'd seen a diagram describing that position in the book of ante-natal exercises she'd bought for Meredith. The caption said it was the most relaxed position there was and that if you lay like that and breathed slowly and deeply, sleep would quickly follow. George breathed in and out, the out part sounding like a very sad sigh, and consciously let the tension out of her body. It was a long time since she'd had a sleepless night. She thought back, and could only remember the endless nights before Sara was born when she had lain awake rigid and squirming with longing for Jos. She couldn't re-create the sensation. That part of her was satisfied, or dead. She smiled as she remembered her fears that she was a sex maniac. Some maniac. She hadn't an atom of lust left after a bare three months, and somehow she couldn't imagine ever feeling that way again, because she couldn't love anyone as she had loved Jos.

I loved Jos. I love Jos. She gave up the relaxed position that only made her body ache, and turned flat on her back. She didn't know if either was true. She'd wanted him, now she didn't care. It wasn't that she did *not* want him, anyway. She was just apathetic. She felt sorry for him, especially when she thought of how lonely he would be. He was supposed to devote himself to enjoying life, yet she didn't think she'd ever seen him doing that for longer than a day.

It was a good thing they had never married, even for Sara's sake. They really weren't suited. Only in contrast to Meredith had she seemed the ideal girl for him, and he, in contrast to no one, had glittered. Their compatibility hadn't stretched further than liking the same food. She had admired him for qualities he'd never possessed, and she would only have made them both miserable by trying to create them in him.

She thought how he had been against them taking Sara, something so right and natural and inevitable. He'd said she would always be between them, that she'd wreck their marriage almost before it had begun. He'd been right, but not because Sara was his daughter and not hers, but because she'd become part of her flesh and blood and not his. He had no feelings for the baby. No pride, no excitement in her, no devotion to the mere fact of her existence. She didn't think he'd foreseen how Sara would become an extension of her, how she would adore and think and live and breathe this baby daughter of his. He'd thought she would look after her through a sense of duty, that she would come between them in the sense that she was a burden.

There was no point in lying on so wide awake. She put the light on, closing her eyes against the sudden orange brilliance. Beside the bed, she had a matinée jacket she was knitting for Sara. She took it up, examining the lumpy stretch of material anxiously. No one had taught her how to knit. The actual knitting and purling were easy, but casting on and off and increasing were giving her a lot of trouble. Still, Sara wouldn't notice the mistakes and she liked doing it. It made her feel she was trying.

She thought she must look something like the grandmother in Red Riding Hood as she sat up in bed with one of Sara's shawls round her shoulders and her big glasses slipping to the end of her nose because of the angle she was sitting at. Anyone would laugh if they came in, not that anyone was going to. She began humming a lullaby until she became too aware of why she was doing it. The slight noise didn't drive anything out of her head, it only made her feel ridiculous and pathetic.

Really, she hadn't guessed how she would react to Sara either, even though she had thought so much about her. She had never imagined love for a baby, especially a baby that wasn't yours, could be so strong and emotional. When she'd held her for the first time, there was a physical sensation not unlike one of desire. The same weak feeling in her stomach, the same breathless anticipation. She hadn't noticed how absorbed she had become in Sara and everything to do with her until she was her willing slave, bound hand and foot.

At the back of her mind, without knowing the exact day, she'd been vaguely conscious that she'd lost interest in Jos. He was an interruption in her relationship with Sara, a figure who came and went and didn't share in anything. She'd probably wanted him to go for some time.

As she confessed this to herself, she felt uneasy. It was like speaking ill of the dead, bringing with it a superstitious dread that the words would rebound upon her disastrously. There was going to be a return to endless hours spent thinking as well as longing, she saw, so she had better get herself in hand. In the old days, before Jos and Sara or any of that, her broodings had always led to the same miserable conclusion, the unhappy realization that she was the unluckiest and most unfortunate girl in the world, and floods of tears. She couldn't see all that returning. Her mind might slip back occasionally to Jos, the way it was doing now, but she felt placid about the prospect. She had Sara and a future. What was more, she had had and rejected all the other things she had ever wanted, like sex and a man and what was exactly the same as marriage. It just wasn't true that to have and to lose, or give up, was worse than never having at all.

Coming to the end of one section of the pattern, she came on to something she couldn't understand. The hieroglyphics meant nothing. She would have to take it down to Peg in the morning, even if she didn't relish the prospect of actually seeking her company. Peg had nothing. So much had happened to her, and at the end of it all she had Sara, but nothing had happened to

Peg. The same old nothing too. It wasn't nice to have Peg around, not that it ever had been in one sense. It ought to make her feel happy because she was so well off and Peg so badly off, but it didn't. She felt nervous in Peg's presence.

She turned the light off and resolved to try to go to sleep again. There was a lot to be done when the real morning came. She had it all planned out. First, she would have to go round to James's and ask her mother if Sara could be left downstairs in the kitchen while she taught upstairs. Then she would have to contact all her former pupils, or rather their mothers and schools, and try to explain her absence as best she could. With luck, they wouldn't have bothered to find anyone else. She must also make very discreet inquiries about how she could become Sara's legal guardian. If she gave too much information away, some busybody might turn up and take the baby away. That she refused to think about. It was a nightmare she must push right to the very back of her mind and pretend didn't exist. She wasn't used to such self-denial. All her nightmares previously had been seized on at regular intervals, gloated over masochistically, and not put back until every drop of pessimistic misery had been squeezed out of them. Now, this one must be treated quite differently, different from the thought of dying which before had been her most nerve-wracking one, never gone into too deeply. Neither Meredith nor Jos wanted, or would ever want, Sara. She had nothing to fear from anyone else. Full stop, full stop.

In the end, George did sleep, for a couple of hours. This time Sara woke her up, and she sprang to look after her, grateful for all the activity that would chase away any thinking. She followed the routine of feeding, bathing and changing with pleasure and satisfaction, and looked with pride on her charge when she was settled in her pram and ready to go out.

It was too far to walk all the way to James's, so she had to invest in a taxi. The taxi driver was very helpful about taking the pram to bits and putting the carry cot part in the back seat. He said Sara was the spitting image of George. George said nothing, only hoping his gushing meant a reasonable fare. When they arrived at James's, she asked him to carry the cot to the doorstep and lean the pram frame against the wall. There was no point in setting it all up again until they were inside. She rang the bell, even though she had her own key and could have let herself in, because she felt a bit of an intruder.

Doris looked up at George and down at the baby.

'No,' said George, 'it isn't. It's Meredith's.'

'I didn't think it was yours,' said Doris. The relief showed plainly in her face. 'Where's Meredith then?'

'Can I come in?' George said. She pushed the frame into the hall and set it up. Doris helped her lift the cot on to it.

'She's a lovely baby,' said Doris. 'Are you going to put her in the garden?'

'Yes,' said George, and wheeled the pram through the hall and into the back. She put the hood up to keep off the wind, and went down the basement steps into the kitchen.

'Well,' said Doris.

'I know,' said George. 'I forgot all about everything.'

'What've you been up to?' asked Doris. 'Your father didn't say much.'

'There isn't much to say,' said George. 'I've been looking after Jos, and the baby.'

'Why couldn't Meredith look after them,' objected Doris, 'she can't have been in hospital all this time, surely?'

'She left,' said George. 'I don't know where she went, so it's no good asking.'

'Left? Left where?' said Doris. 'You don't mean she left her husband and that baby?'

'That's right,' said George.

'Well,' said Doris, and then, 'How's he going to manage with a baby?'

'I don't know,' said George.

'George,' said Doris, 'you haven't let yourself be landed looking after them two?'

'No,' said George, 'only the baby. Sara.'

Doris stared. 'Not for keeps,' she said, flatly.

'Yes,' said George.

'Oh don't talk silly,' said Doris, in a sudden burst of temper.

'You've had some daft ideas but this beats the band. I've never heard of anything so ridiculous and – and *stupid* in all my born days. What do you know about babies? Think of its future – you've nothing to offer it, nothing.'

'I've got myself,' murmured George.

'Don't be soft,' snapped Doris. 'That's soft talk, you're not right in the head carrying on like that. I don't know what you're thinking of.'

'The baby,' said George simply.

'Then it's time somebody told you a few home truths,' said Doris.

'Such as?' said George. She'd expected all this.

'You're not fit to bring up a child. You're not married and never likely to be with a ready-made baby round your neck, apart from anything else. You haven't any money, nor a proper home, and no security at all. You ought to be ashamed of yourself even thinking about it.'

'I'd look after it better than a Dr Barnardo's Home or somewhere,' said George.

'I'd like five minutes with its proper mother and father,' said Doris.

'That wouldn't do much good. They don't want it,' said George.

'They should have thought about that before they had it,' said Doris.

'Obviously,' George agreed.

'The poor little thing,' sighed Doris. 'It's a shame.'

'I know,' said George. 'I feel so sorry for her. None of this is her fault.'

They were silent for a minute, united in the heartbreaking thought of Sara's pathos.

'All the same,' said Doris, though with a slight change of tone. 'It wouldn't be right for you to keep her. You mustn't think of it.'

'I can't help it,' pleaded George.

'You'll just have to help it,' said Doris firmly, 'you won't get a man and a baby of your own that way.'

'I don't want a man or any other baby except Sara,' said George. 'There isn't any point talking about it.'

'What have you come here for then?' said Doris, abruptly. 'I'll have no hand in it.'

'I want you to look after Sara while I give lessons here,' said George. 'I'll pay you.'

'I don't want to be paid,' said Doris. 'I don't know how you could suggest it. I won't, anyway.'

'It would only be for a few hours,' said George. 'She's no trouble, really.'

'That's nothing to do with it,' said Doris. 'No.'

'All right,' said George, 'I'll have to put her in a nursery. It doesn't really make much difference, it would have been handier, that's all.'

Doris set her lips, grimly. She wasn't going to be got round. 'They'll ask questions at any nursery,' she warned, 'and then you'll cop it. They'll soon find out you're not fit to bring up a child.'

'What do you mean – "fit",' shouted George, 'I'm sick of hearing you say it. I'm not a crook, or blind or anything. I don't go around drinking or swearing or gambling. You'd think I was a prostitute the way you're talking. I'm perfectly fit.'

'It's no good shouting,' said Doris. 'You're not married.'

'What's so marvellous about being married?' yelled George. 'You'd think only married people were human, or had a pre-rogative on decency. Meredith was married and she didn't even want her baby. There are some lousy married mothers and some wonderful unmarried ones.'

'Exactly,' said Doris. 'That's what people would think. They'd see a single girl with a baby and there you are.'

'Oh God,' stormed George, 'Who cares what people think?'

'Sara, or whatever you call her, might,' said Doris. 'People might say things to her. You haven't thought of that.'

'It wouldn't matter,' protested George. 'It would be so easy to explain everything. Sara would know the truth right from the beginning.'

'Would she?' said Doris.

For some reason she didn't understand, George's heart began to beat very fast, as though she were afraid.

'All she would understand,' said Doris, 'would be that everyone else had a father as well as a mother.'

'Widows' children have the same problem,' said George. 'It would be no worse than being in a home and having neither.'

'Yes it would,' said Doris. 'There, everyone would be the same. That matters to children.' George was silent. 'You want to think of yourself,' warned Doris.

'I have,' said George. 'I'm not being noble. I know what it would mean, but it would all be worth it.'

'Suppose a man came along when Sara was seven or eight,' said Doris.

'He won't,' said George. 'And anyway even supposing, just to please you, that he did, I wouldn't be interested in anyone who didn't want Sara.'

'That's what you say now,' said Doris. 'I've heard that before.'

'It's no good arguing,' said George, 'I've made my mind up. I'm sorry I bothered you. Where's the nearest nursery in this stinking neighbourhood? I bet they don't have L.C.C. nurseries, they're too bloody posh.'

'I don't know, I'm sure,' said Doris. 'Aren't you moving a bit quick?'

'Why?' said George.

'Things have changed here, though you may have been too busy to give a thought to that,' said Doris sarcastically. 'Mr James might not be willing to let you have that room for your classes. I suppose you hadn't thought of that.'

George stared at her.

'No, I hadn't,' she said blankly. 'Why should he object?'

'His new wife might not like it,' said Doris.'

'His new what?' said George.

'Wife.'

'He can't be married,' said George. She was going to say that he would have asked her first, but thought better of it. 'When did he get married? Nobody told me.'

'Why should they?' said Doris, tartly. 'You haven't shown any interest in his affairs up to now, not even coming to the funeral like that.'

'What's she like?' asked George. 'Where did he meet her? How long has he known her?'

'It's no good asking me,' said Doris. 'I've never even seen her and I don't know anything about her. She'll be like the last one, I expect. Whatever she's like, it'll be an end to the nice easy ways of the last few weeks that's certain.'

'Doesn't she live here?' said George. 'I mean, if you haven't seen her. Are they on their honeymoon?'

'They aren't married yet,' said Doris. 'He's just told us, that's all. He came out with it weeks ago and we've been waiting ever since. He can't spend much time with her anyway, he's never been out. Your father did ask him when the happy day was to be, but he never gave a proper answer. Real secretive, he is. Sits there and says "we'll see" and that's all.'

George felt a rush of relief, and was ashamed of herself. She hadn't given a thought to James ever since her affair with Jos had begun. He belonged to a farcical episode in the past which one day she would laugh about with Jos. She hadn't even bothered to give him the answer he had so dramatically demanded, because when she'd found Jos it had seemed so ludicrous that there was any answer to be given. Somehow she'd expected him to realize that. Now hearing about his intended new wife, she felt unreasonably annoyed, as though he had no right to be interested in any woman except her. It made even more of a fool out of her, somehow.

'Is James in now?' she said.

'No,' said Doris. 'I don't know where he is, but I don't expect he's gone far. Ask your father. He's in the dining room polishing the silver.'

George wandered off to find Ted. He had all the silver spread out on a thick, green, baize cloth at one end of the table – one pile to his left, dull with the polish he'd put on, and another to his right, gleaming from the friction of his soft, yellow duster. He was wearing a dark blue apron, with the strings brought twice round his middle and tied in a bow at the front. She thought he looked very old and sulky.

'Hello, dad,' she said, and sat down at the table, idly picking up one of the polished forks and twisting it round and round to catch the light.

'Give me that,' said Ted, snatching it away. 'I've just cleaned it. You don't want to go making marks all over it.'

'Sorry,' said George. 'Is this in honour of the new Mrs Leamington?'

'I clean the silver once a month as you very well know,' said Ted sharply. 'This is my silver-cleaning morning, that's all.' He looked up. 'If you've just come to make trouble,' he said, 'you can go away again.'

'It was a joke,' said George.

'I don't like them sort of jokes,' said Ted, viciously polishing the handle of a knife.

George kept quiet, watching him. She could imagine his delight at Mrs L.'s death. He must have been in sole control of James all these weeks, relishing his dependence upon him. It was all to go. James would be a zealous and devoted husband for a time, and Ted couldn't know what humiliations might lie ahead. James needing to get married he would see as a betrayal, some slight upon himself. There would be no question of leaving his service whatever the new Mrs L. was like, indeed no, that was what must make it all so worrying.

'Never mind, dad,' said George suddenly. 'She might not be so bad.'

'What you getting at?' said Ted, furiously.

'The new Mrs L.,' said George, 'she might not bas bad as the last one.'

'I don't know what you're driving at,' said Ted, 'but you mind your own business. If Mr James chooses to get married again then it's a very good thing. He's in the prime of life isn't he? What's more natural? You just watch what you're saying if you're going to come round here again my girl. That's all.'

George got up and went up to her music room. The key was on the outside, but the door was locked. She turned it, and went in. The room had an overpoweringly musty smell. The piano had a fine coating of dust and the mirror was covered with a thin film of dirt. She was surprised it had such a neglected air after so short a time.

She went over to the windows and pulled them both wide open, drawing back the curtains as far as they would go to let as much air as possible in. With her scarf, she dusted the piano and opened it. Instead of automatically thumping out some tune, her fingers hovered uncertainly over the keys, not knowing which notes to strike. The last time she had played was before Sara was born, when she'd had everything before her and not known it. She had played then, discontented and frustrated, thinking of all the empty, useless hours surrounding her. This room had seen her crying there in the mirror, dejected and miserable, full of a restlessness that she could find no outlet for. It was gone. She felt quiet, sad, but she wasn't unhappy. Slowly, she began to play a lullaby for Sara, smiling slushily at herself in the mirror.

The sound of the piano was what James had been waiting for. He came in from his club in time for lunch, and heard the music from outside, standing on his doorstep. Gently, he let himself in, hoping Ted wouldn't hear and come rushing out, spoiling everything. He'd known that sooner or later she would come back, without him asking or doing anything to make her. Whatever she'd been doing would come to an end and she would be driven back to that room.

He opened the door very quietly and stepped inside, pushing it to behind him. She looked up immediately.

'Don't stop playing,' he said.

George felt herself blushing violently. 'I wasn't really playing anything,' she said. She was afraid he would make some heavy joke about her answer.

'It sounded very nice to me,' said James. And then, 'you look different. What have you been doing to yourself?'

'Nothing really,' said George, peeking at herself in the mirror. She looked exactly the same. 'Oh, by the way,' she said, 'I was very sorry to hear about your wife's death.'

'Were you?' said James steadily.

'Of course,' said George, 'it was just that I was very busy at the time. That's no excuse, but really I was sorry.'

'I wasn't,' said James. He walked over towards her, and stood beside the piano with his arms clasped behind him. 'It was a shock at first, naturally,' he said, 'and I don't like death and all that business. But I wasn't sorry, not when I realized it meant I was free.'

'My mother told me,' said George. 'I didn't know you were getting married again.'

'You should have done,' said James.

'Why, do I know her?' said George, frowning and trying to recollect the silly women who had fluttered around James.

'Come off it,' said James. 'You're the one I'm going to marry.'

George felt that every atom of scarlet blood in her had rushed into her face, into every nook and cranny. She gasped, as though she was choking, and put her hand up to her mouth.

'You never gave me an answer,' James was saying. 'Well of course I see now it was a damn silly proposition for a girl like you. I think it's very much to your credit that you didn't lower yourself by replying. I'd have done the same. Mind you, I'm still sure it would have worked out, but it wouldn't have been ideal. You're the sort that wants the ideal, no half measures or messing about. It's all or nothing, isn't it, even if it looked as though nothing was more likely? I've had a lot of time to think it all out in the last few weeks and I can see my mistake was never mentioning that I might marry you. You couldn't know I was serious without me doing that. Well, it's all quite straightforward now, we can get married when you like.'

George turned away from him, unable to take in quite what he was saying with his dominating body bang in front of her. He's got a kink, she thought, he really has. He talks as though we had been passionate lovers, as though we'd had some longstanding affair. She wondered if Mrs L.'s death had turned his brain.

'A lot's happened to me too,' she said, 'since I saw you. It's not as if things were the same, even.'

'I sent your father round,' James said. 'I thought something was going on.'

'I had an affair,' said George, shyly. 'You might not think it, but I did. A love affair.'

163

'It didn't work out,' stated James.

'No. It didn't, but it changes everything.'

'Why?' said James.

George thought that a few months ago she could have told him brutally why, she could have said that the only reason she'd shown any interest in him, such as it was, was because she was man mad. She wanted somebody of her own, to make love to her, she was that desperate, or she would have laughed in his face.

'I've got a baby to look after, my friends',' she said. 'Her parents didn't want her.'

'That's all right,' said James. 'You know how I feel about children. She'll give our family a good start, the more the merrier.'

Looking up at him, George thought how that was the reaction she'd wanted from Jos, but it never came. James had some feeling then. She believed he really did welcome Sara and wasn't just saying it to persuade her. He would make a good father. She wasn't likely to fall in love with anyone, after Jos. She didn't have any illusions to get rid of.

It was a good solution to her problem, if only James wasn't so repulsive. She said the word to herself and tried to analyse why she didn't like him. Perhaps it was just the backlog of all the years of that false relationship her father had foisted on to them. In any case, all her emotions except her love for Sara seemed dulled and unimportant. She could get over dislike.

Still playing with the idea, only toying, she said: 'I don't love you.'

'I never expected you to,' said James, 'I told you that.'

'I'm not interested in sex any more either,' said George. 'Gone right off it, I 'ave,' she added, trying to pick up the threads of her old bitter, bright little cracks.

'We'll see about that,' said James.

'I don't think I can have children either,' said George. 'I think I'm sterile, or barren to put it in biblical terms.'

A shade of caution passed over James's face.

'How do you know?' he said.

'That's put you off,' said George. 'I don't know, I only think. I didn't become pregnant all those weeks with Jos, and he's not sterile.'

'Doesn't prove anything,' said James.

'No. Do you want me to be examined?' said George. She suddenly thought she would like to be examined and know.

'Not yet,' said James, 'give it a chance first.'

George closed her eyes self-consciously and tried to tell herself the whole thing was utterly pathetic. He was marrying her now out of loneliness, not for any twisted psychological reason. She was handy and accessible. And she was marrying him for security and ease and babies, babies she would probably never have. It would be the most negative marriage of all time.

She didn't ask for time to think about it. There wasn't much thinking to do. The alternatives were well known to her, she'd been over and over them ever since Jos walked out, and she didn't like them. So much of what her mother had said was true, she had no right to bring up Sara to the sort of narrow life she would be able to offer. It would be awful having to live with a sentimental, self-pitying spinster who used you as a vicarious substitute for the love and marriage and children she'd never had. I might even keep telling her how grateful she ought to be, George thought. It would be better to be the adopted child of a business marriage, definitely. The pretence of normality would be so much easier.

'All right,' she said, 'it's a deal.'

'Good,' James wasn't offended by the way she'd phrased it. 'Good,' he said again, and smiled. 'You won't regret it,' he promised.

They stayed where they were. It was difficult to know what to do. James took a deep breath.

'We'll have a white wedding,' he said, 'in a church. People can say what they like.'

'Anything you like,' said George, 'but I'll look a bloody sight tarted up in white.'

'You'll look beautiful,' said James. 'I've often imagined how you would look. Don't you worry.'

'I'm not worried,' said George. 'I'm just warning you, mate.'

165

'We'll go to the Bahamas for our honeymoon,' said James.

'I can't leave Sara,' said George. Defensively, she waited for him to ask who Sara was, or to remonstrate about taking a baby on a honeymoon.

'We'll take her with us,' said James, 'and a nanny to look after her if you like.'

'I don't like,' said George, frowning. 'I look after her.'

'Right,' said James. 'That's settled. We'll get married in a month's time, give us time to do things properly.'

'One thing,' said George. 'My mother and father. I don't want them around when we are married. You can sack them.'

'Ted?' said James, perturbed. 'What would he do?'

'That's something he should have found out for himself a long time ago,' said George.

'I'll pension him off, handsomely,' said James.

'You can do what you like, as long as he isn't here to kow-tow to you when we get back,' said George firmly.

'He's my friend,' said James.

'I'll be your wife,' said George. 'You don't need both. Anyway, he isn't your friend. He loathes your guts, and so does Doris.'

'I can't believe that,' said James.

'Of course you can't,' said George. 'You're much too conceited and weak.'

James chuckled, and then laughed loudly. 'That's my Georgy girl,' he roared, slapping George on the shoulder.

'It is indeed,' said George, dryly.

Eventually, they went into the garden so that George could display Sara to her prospective father. It was a highly successful meeting. James picked her up and made a fool of himself, and Sara gurgled appreciatively and slightly sarcastically. Then they went inside and George told her mother and father, who were having their lunch in the kitchen, that she was going to marry James. She said it straight out, without any preamble. They couldn't tell her not to be stupid or disrespectful because James was standing at her side, beaming his approval.

Ted had to sit down very quickly.

George knew nothing would be said until she was on her own. She made James sit down, there and then, at the kitchen table and told Doris that as he was now one of the family he could eat with them. James thought that was a very good joke. Ted was nearly sick with horror and embarrassment. When they'd finished an almost silent meal, George thought it time she got it over and sent James off to take Sara for a walk in the park. He departed docilely, even proudly.

'You can start,' George said, the minute he'd gone, 'who's going to shoot first?'

'I don't know what you mean,' said Doris, tightly. 'We've nothing to say except what's been said. We hope you'll be very happy.'

'And dad?' said George.

'Leave him alone,' said Doris.

'I bet he doesn't hope we'll be happy,' said George. 'I bet he hopes I rot in hell and James comes running back to him.' Ted still said nothing. 'Come on, dad. Say Mr James can't be wrong, whatever he does is wonderful.'

'You don't care about him,' said Ted slowly, without looking up from the empty table.

'No,' said George. 'I don't. I'm marrying him for sheer security and because I can't be bothered to do anything else. We can't all love him like you – but then I don't hate him either.'

'Who said anything about hate?' said Doris fearfully.

George ignored her. 'It will be the best thing that ever happened to you both, me marrying James,' she said. 'He's going to pension you off, I asked him to. You'll have to move away and make your own life and you'll only see him once a week when you come to tea. Then maybe you'll both get straightened out and won't have wasted absolutely all your lives.'

She wanted Ted to get very angry, to shout at her. A first class row would show him up for what he was. But he didn't rise to her taunts. He remained at the table, head bowed, not even telling her to be quiet. As soon as she saw his submission, she felt sorry. He was too weak and useless to attack, he was just a prop.

Doris kept her argument to herself. She didn't know if it was true about being pensioned off, and, after wanting such a break for years, she now found that she didn't care. Her words to George about not being capable of bringing up Sara, and never finding a man, came back to her. Perhaps they'd goaded her daughter into accepting James. She, too, couldn't understand this new situation, but not, like Ted, because she couldn't understand a marriage without love on at least the woman's part. She understood that very well. It was what must have happened in the past that mystified her. James wasn't a man of impulse, everything was always planned. She tried to remember any occasion on which he'd shown a partiality for George, but could conjure up none. He'd always treated her scrupulously like a daughter, of that she was sure. It was disgusting of him to marry her. It made a mockery of all those past years. George, of course, didn't care. He was a husband. She was taking what she could get, and she was lucky at that.

George left all the arrangements to James. She went for dress fittings where and when she was ordered and glowered at herself in the mirrors of the establishment he chose. She would look an absolute clown, but that was his affair. He pleased her, however, by insisting that Sara should be formally adopted by them. She had no idea how to go about this, but James told her to leave it all to his solicitor. The only part she played was giving him Jos's poste restante address. She didn't think he would object.

The day before she was married, she finally moved out of her flat. Peg moved in. She couldn't understand why Peg should want to do this, but from the minute she'd announced her departure, Peg had said she would like her flat.

'Why?' George asked, blankly.

'It's bigger,' said Peg.

'But there's only you,' said George. 'What do you want a bigger flat for? What will you do with all the space?'

'Spread out,' said Peg, promptly. 'I'm cramped down there.'

'It's twice your rent,' said George. 'How will you afford six pounds instead of three? It's ridiculous.'

'T'isn't,' said Peg. 'I don't spend much. I don't go out or buy clothes. I've just got my rent and food and something for a rainy day. There's no point in saving for nothing.'

George shrugged. She didn't want Peg in her flat. She wanted to leave it bare and empty and see a stranger move in.

'You could always come back,' said Peg. George stared at her blankly. 'If you leave that man,' said Peg, 'you and Sara could move in with me.'

'Why should you think I'd leave him?' said George. 'I haven't even married him yet.'

'You might have married Jos,' said Peg, 'and you left him.'

'He left me.'

'Same thing. You were alone anyway. That's all I meant. If you end up alone there's always a place for you here.'

'Thanks,' said George, choking. It sounded like her epitaph.

When Peg's prize curtains were up and her massive bed in place, the flat had changed completely. George felt bound to help her make the move, and patiently toiled up and down the stairs with her goods and chattels. If Peg was wild with delight, none of it showed.

'We'll have a cup of tea,' said Peg at five o'clock. 'You'll have to go now I expect.'

'Yes,' said George. 'I suppose I'd better.'

'Is your wedding dress nice?' said Peg, filling the kettle.

'Oh, ravishing,' said George.

'I never thought you'd get married,' said Peg. 'It seems funny somehow.'

'Have a good laugh, then, for God's sake,' said George.

'I thought you'd be like me,' said Peg. 'Funny how it's turned out you getting two men.'

'You mean in spite of my ugly mug?' said George, savagely.

'Well, you know,' said Peg. 'It seems queer. Do you like this James?'

'No,' said George.

'He's old enough to be your father, isn't he?' said Peg.

'Madam, he is my father,' said George.

'You're joking,' said Peg, uncertainly.

'No, I'm not,' said George, 'he's my father and Jos was my brother so you see it's all explained.'

'I shall enjoy the wedding,' said Peg.

'It will be good entertainment,' agreed George, 'ices in the interval and everything. Mind you're early and get a seat in the stalls. You don't want to miss any of the best bits.'

Peg was early. She arrived at the church half an hour before anyone else, wearing a new blue hat and her Hebe costume. George's side hadn't many guests so she was the fourth row, nearest to the aisle, with a splendid view of everything. She settled down comfortably, reading her favourite hymns and sucking a mint very discreetly in time to the music in her head. She didn't think much of George's choice of hymns. You could tell the bride hadn't been in a church for years when she chose 'O Perfect Love' which had a rotten tune. She'd have chosen something easy and rousing, herself.

When the guests began to arrive, Peg put down her hymn book and swallowed the last bit of her mint. She didn't know any of the people, of course, which spoiled it a bit, but she enjoyed staring at everybody with no one knowing who she was either. It was obvious who George's mother was. She was wearing floral blue silk and had a very stiff face. Peg felt sorry for her. She could feel there was no proper wedding atmosphere, nobody whispered or smiled or nodded at anyone else. It was more like a funeral.

She studied James carefully when he took up his seat on the right hand front side. She was surprised he'd turned out so good looking. He was a bit fat, but not so that you couldn't call it heavy built. He was very straight backed with black hair, grey at the temples, and she thought he had a kind face. He was very smart.

Peg was the only one who turned right round to stare blatantly at the bride as she started on the long walk down the aisle. She looks ever so nice, Peg thought. They'd done something queer with her hair, twisted it all in coils on top of her head. Regal looking, that was the phrase. The dress was beautiful, high necked, long sleeved and masses of skirt. Easy ten yards in that skirt alone.

She came past Peg, on her father's arm, and Peg could see she was quite flushed. Not what you'd call red, but sort of pink. It was becoming. Peg was very impressed, she'd never thought George would turn out so well.

After the services, which went off very nicely, Peg went home. She'd decided not to go to the reception because she wouldn't know anybody and it would be awkward. Better to go home and have some tea by herself, and a quiet think about how nice George had looked and how happy she must be and about her honeymoon and house and Sara and perhaps other children, and how there was no knowing what might turn up for oneself.

Discover more about our forthcoming books through Penguin's FREE newspaper...

Penguin Quarterly

It's packed with:

- exciting features
- author interviews
- previews & reviews
- books from your favourite films & TV series
- exclusive competitions & much, much more...

Write off for your free copy today to:
Dept JC
Penguin Books Ltd
FREEPOST
West Drayton
Middlesex
UB7 0BR
NO STAMP REQUIRED

READ MORE IN PENGUIN

In every corner of the world, on every subject under the sun, Penguin represents quality and variety – the very best in publishing today.

For complete information about books available from Penguin – including Puffins, Penguin Classics and Arkana – and how to order them, write to us at the appropriate address below. Please note that for copyright reasons the selection of books varies from country to country.

In the United Kingdom: Please write to *Dept. JC, Penguin Books Ltd, FREEPOST, West Drayton, Middlesex UB7 OBR*

If you have any difficulty in obtaining a title, please send your order with the correct money, plus ten per cent for postage and packaging, to *PO Box No. 11, West Drayton, Middlesex UB7 OBR*

In the United States: Please write to *Penguin USA Inc., 375 Hudson Street, New York, NY 10014*

In Canada: Please write to *Penguin Books Canada Ltd, 10 Alcorn Avenue, Suite 300, Toronto, Ontario M4V 3B2*

In Australia: Please write to *Penguin Books Australia Ltd, 487 Maroondah Highway, Ringwood, Victoria 3134*

In New Zealand: Please write to *Penguin Books (NZ) Ltd, 182–190 Wairau Road, Private Bag, Takapuna, Auckland 9*

In India: Please write to *Penguin Books India Pvt Ltd, 706 Eros Apartments, 56 Nehru Place, New Delhi 110 019*

In the Netherlands: Please write to *Penguin Books Netherlands B.V., Keizersgracht 231 NL–1016 DV Amsterdam*

In Germany: Please write to *Penguin Books Deutschland GmbH, Friedrichstrasse 10–12, W–6000 Frankfurt/Main 1*

In Spain: Please write to *Penguin Books S. A., C. San Bernardo 117–6° E–28015 Madrid*

In Italy: Please write to *Penguin Italia s.r.l., Via Felice Casati 20, I–20124 Milano*

In France: Please write to *Penguin France S. A., 17 rue Lejeune, F–31000 Toulouse*

In Japan: Please write to *Penguin Books Japan, Ishikiribashi Building, 2–5–4, Suido, Tokyo 112*

In Greece: Please write to *Penguin Hellas Ltd, Dimocritou 3, GR–106 71 Athens*

In South Africa: Please write to *Longman Penguin Southern Africa (Pty) Ltd, Private Bag X08, Bertsham 2013*

BY THE SAME AUTHOR

The Battle for Christabel

Rowena wants a baby. What she doesn't want is the baby's father. Yet five years after the birth of Christabel, Rowena is dead, tragically killed in a climbing accident. The battle for Christabel has begun . . .

'Forster has the essential capacity to see everyone's point of view, whether it is the social workers who resent the upper-middle class assumptions of Christabel's grandmother, Isobel's lover who believes she should adopt the child, or Christabel's foster mother Betty . . . in that territory of dread and reconciliation which is the family, Forster reigns supreme' – *Guardian*

'Poignant, impeccably written . . . especially heart-rending because it is so believable' – *Company*

Lady's Maid

'Compulsively readable . . . at each climax of the story, from the Brownings' runaway romance to her own equally compromised and complicated marriage, the lady's maid speaks directly and at the last most movingly' – *Guardian*. 'Fact and fiction are skilfully interwoven . . . beautifully done' – *Evening Standard*

also published

Mother Can You Hear Me?
Private Papers
Have the Men Had Enough?
The Seduction of Mrs Pendlebury

and

Significant Sisters
The Grassroots of Active Feminism 1839–1939